GRIZZLY GRIEVANCE

PET WHISPERER P.I.
BOOK 13

MOLLY FITZ

ABOUT THIS BOOK

Life has been kind of hectic lately, so Charles and I have decided to fill our weekend with the three Rs: Rest, Relaxation, and Romance, courtesy of a private weekend away.

Unsurprisingly, two furry stowaways manage to sneak aboard our rental RV, which means we're stuck with one very bossy talking cat and a raccoon who's decided to role-play the weekend as some kind of big rig trucker.

And if that wasn't enough to put a damper on things, the dead body that shows up in the communal picnic area surely does the trick.

Throw in a grizzly mama with a desperate plea for us to help find her cubs, a budding reality TV star who's desperate to be liked by everyone she meets, and a couple secrets of our own, and the four of us are in for one wild, wild weekend!

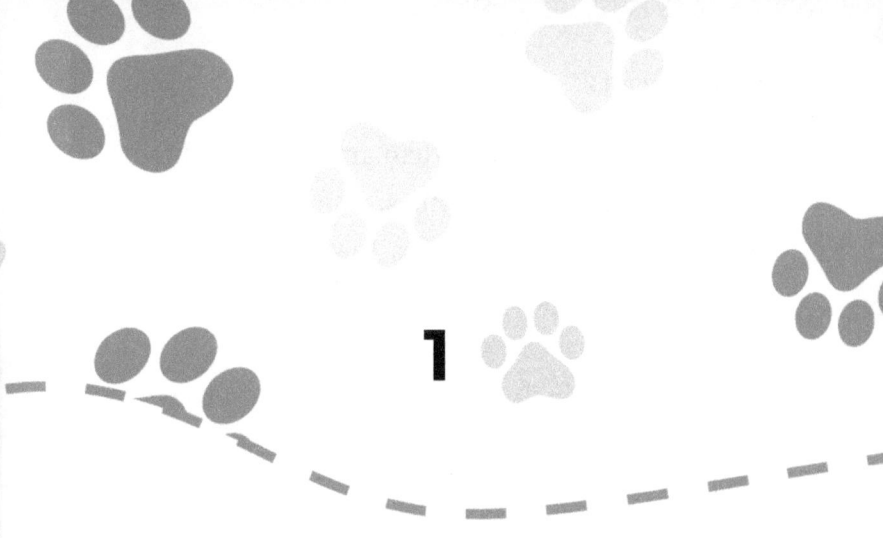

'm Angie Russo, and lately my life has been one train wreck after another. And, yeah, I do mean that literally. First my cat and I found ourselves aboard a derailed train about six months back, and then just a couple weeks ago, my nan crashed her sports car on the highway with us in it.

I've started to fear various modes of transportation just as much as I've feared electric coffee makers for a while now. In my life, both have only led to trouble.

And that's how it all started, too.

I got zapped by an old coffee maker and woke up with the strange new ability to talk to animals. And those talking animals have led to most of my problems, like the aforementioned vehicle wrecks.

I've also dealt with more than anyone's fair share of murders, thefts, kidnappings, and other nefarious crimes. Then again, I guess that's what I get for setting up shop as a private investigator.

Still...

I could really do with just a week or two where nothing life-altering comes around and rocks my world.

I can't even remember the last time I enjoyed a good old-fashioned Netflix binge or spent the full day in bed reading. Also, I almost never get paid for my investigative work, which begs the question: Why do I keep signing myself up for more and more?

My partner at Pet Whisperer P.I. has zero issues saying no. Of course, he's not the one doing any of the talking. He wouldn't miss napping in a sunbeam or giving himself a slow, leisurely tongue bath for anything... Oh, did I mention my partner is a cat?

He's a standard tabby with an oversized attitude, but don't tell him I said that. His full name is Octavius Maxwell Ricardo Edmund Frederick Fulton Russo, Esq, P.I. (a name he freely and regularly adds to). I prefer to call him Octo-Cat. He's not a fan, but at least he's stopped arguing with me about it.

The trust fund his previous owner left him pays all our bills, and those rare moments when he offers me genuine displays of love and affection are the brightest spots in my day.

We also live in our—or rather his—giant manor house alongside my nan and her rescue Chihuahua, Paisley. Pringle the nosy reality TV addict lives in a treehouse in our backyard; he's a raccoon. And then we have Charles, my big-time lawyer boyfriend, to round out our motley crew.

Our latest adventure took Nan, Octo-Cat, Paisley, and me on a cross-country trip to visit my cat's girlfriend, a former show Himalayan named Grizabella. On the way, I learned that Nan has been blabbing what is meant to be a secret ability to random friends of hers on the Internet.

While that was going on, a militarized flock of seagulls bribed me into helping with their turf dispute, a case that mainly fell to Charles and Pringle since the rest of us were out of town.

And even though we held up our end of the bargain, the seagulls needed more time to deliver on theirs. I trust them, though. Any day now, they'll lead me to my long-lost grandmother and I'll finally learn the truth about my lineage.

Until then, I've been doing my best to focus on other things. It hasn't been going well...

Mainly because my cat makes non-stop demands, and I'm just too tired to argue with him anymore. That's why I'm driving more than thirty minutes out to Misty Harbor to purchase a lobster roll from his preferred venue, the Little Dog Diner. And when I get home, he probably won't even say thank you for sending me to another far-flung end of Blueberry Bay to fulfill his latest request.

Yeah...

Have I mentioned just how badly I need a break from my life?

* * *

When I returned that afternoon with a bag of lobster rolls in hand, I found a pair of seagulls roosting on my porch.

"Bravo?" I asked as I parked my car and ambled over to greet them. "And is that Abigull? No way."

The smaller of the two birds puffed out her feathers and let out a tinkling giggle. When I last saw her a few weeks back, she'd been little more than a hatchling. Now she was almost as large as her adoptive father—and a very happy-looking bird at that.

"We've finished our search for your grandmother," Bravo informed me without further pretense. He'd promised to put me in touch with my long-lost biological grandmother in return for Charles, Pringle, and me assisting in a land dispute with another flock. And I knew he was trying his best to deliver on his end of the deal, but the more that time passed, the less I believed any of us would be able to find her.

I never should have doubted them, I realized now as an enormous smile stretched across my face. "That's wonderful. Can you take me to her now?" I moved back toward my car, but the seagulls didn't follow.

"She's not here anymore," Abigull said with a sad shake of her head.

Bravo picked up where his ward left off. "She was here in the Bay for a long time, but now we can't locate her."

"Did she...?" I swallowed hard, unable to believe the horrible timing. "Did she die?"

"Oh gosh no!" The little bird chirped and shifted her weight from foot to foot. "Nothing like that."

"I've put my best gulls on scouting duty, but so far we're unable to locate her new residence," Bravo added, all business, while Abigull seemed much more concerned about tending to my feelings.

"So what now?" I asked with a sigh. I appreciated that they'd tried but also felt terribly heartbroken that I may never get to meet my missing family member after all.

"We'll keep searching, but we'll need to expand the radius. She may have left the state. It's no problem, really. We will find her, but it's just going to take a little longer than originally estimated."

"Thank you," I said, working hard to show them a smile even though the news they'd just brought me had ruined my whole day. "Thank you for not giving up."

"Nothing can stop a bird on a mission," Bravo informed me with a narrowed gaze.

"Yeah," his adoptive daughter chimed in.

"Now we must be off." Bravo immediately launched into the sky with Abigull at his tail.

"Bye, Angie," the girl gull called as they soared away on the winds.

I slumped down onto the worn oak porch steps and sat there for a while, just me and the dwindling warmth of the setting sun.

What would I do if the flock failed to find my grandmother? I'd already questioned my remaining family in Larkhaven, searched every nook and cranny of the Internet... I'd even tried the genealogy route but had come up with absolutely nothing.

Somewhere out there, I had a grandmother I hadn't even known existed until last year. Her entire family had been stolen from her when my grandpa took their baby—my mother—and asked Nan to take her somewhere far away.

None of us knew why, and my grandpa had already passed by the time I learned of his existence. And now these two huge players in my personal history were nothing more than a giant question mark, and I doubted I'd ever really be whole again until I could find her.

2

Octo-Cat found me on the porch a while later. I wasn't sure how much time had passed since the pair of seagulls delivered the news of their delay in finding my family. It must have been a while, though, because the light had faded and a chill that hadn't been there before now hung in the air.

"What are you doing out here?" Octo-Cat asked after pushing through the automatic pet door and coming to sit at my side.

I would have thought he was showing a rare moment of affection, except the next words out of his mouth were, "And where is my lobster roll?"

I sighed and pushed the almost transparent paper bag over to him.

"It's almost all the way cold," he whined as he crinkled his way into the sack, but he accepted the food nonetheless.

I sat and watched the branches of the white ash trees that lined our property as they blew in the wind.

"Do you—uh—want some?" my cat offered hesitantly, his face a distorted mask of concern through the oily paper. His eyes remained glued to the food, daring me to accept the offer.

I shook my head. "All yours."

"You seem..." The bag broke open, spilling the cat and his lobster roll onto the porch with me. He grabbed the food with his paws and tried to regain his normal, dignified air. With a twinkle in his eyes, he turned his head to one side then the other as he examined me. "Less irritating than usual," he decided at last. "What's wrong?"

"Bravo is having a hard time finding my grand-mother." I shrugged, trying to play off my devastation.

"So what's the big deal? You've lived without her this long. Besides, I haven't seen my mother or any of my brothers or sisters since I was a kitten. And you're well past your youth now, Angela."

I chuckled at his logic. "Cats and people aren't

the same. I think you know that better than anyone."

"I've been thinking about that," Octo-Cat said, bits of lobster hanging from his chin and whiskers. "And I spend way too much time with humans and other lesser creatures these days..."

He paused to let this sink in. I assumed the other lesser creatures referred to Paisley and Pringle but knew better than to ask for specifics.

"It might be nice to know what happened to my litter mates," he continued, running a paw over his face. "Ever since we found those kittens, I got to thinking. What if all my brothers and sisters turned out almost as awesome as me?"

"That's hard to believe," I said with another laugh. Leave it to Octo-Cat to make my personal tragedy all about him.

"You're right. It would be almost too amazing, but that's a chance I'm willing to take."

I turned to look at him, cupping my cheek in one palm and resting my elbow on my thigh. "What do you mean?"

He finished chewing his bite and swallowed hard. "We're searching for your family. I want to search for mine, too."

"But—"

"But nothing. I think it's fair to ask, since it is my trust fund that pays all our bills."

"Remember how curiosity killed the cat?" I asked with one eyebrow raised, a slight smile playing at my lips.

Octo-Cat scoffed at this. "That's just a vicious generalization, and you know it. But fine, I am curious. What's so wrong about that?"

He had me there. It was only natural that with all the focus on my family Octo-Cat would also wonder about his.

"Okay," I said, nodding for emphasis. "I'll help you."

"Don't make me pull out my—" He stopped suddenly. "Wait, you'll help? That easily?"

"That easily," I confirmed, my smile widening now.

"Well, okay, then. Thank you." He returned to his lobster roll, making such fast progress of it that I was worried he may choke.

Just then, a raccoon skittered up the porch steps and grabbed the remaining sandwich with greedy black fingers.

Octo-Cat growled and took a swipe, but Pringle had already managed to climb up onto the railing and out of reach of the irate tabby.

"For me?" the raccoon crooned. "Why, Angie, you shouldn't have."

"She didn't!" Octo-cat yelled and flicked his tail wildly behind him.

Pringle stuffed the entire thing in his mouth, cheeks bulging, then swallowed it down and slowly licked each of his fingertips.

"I hate you," Octo-Cat muttered before running back in through the pet door.

I let out a long sigh. "Why do you have to get him riled up like that?"

"That cat has never liked me. So, frankly, I don't trust his taste. Although that lobster roll was delicious. Would have been even more delicious without the cat spit on it, though." Pringle chuckled to himself, then clambered down from the railing and came to sit at my side. "So when do we start our next case?"

I sighed again—something I did often in my raccoon neighbor's presence. "When someone hires us."

"Hey, not being hired hasn't stopped you before. You've gotten involved in plenty of cases just because you happened to stumble upon them. Let's go for a nice walk through downtown, see what trouble we can stir up there."

I stared at him for a moment, but when I realized Pringle had no idea why this suggestion would be problematic, I attempted to explain. "If I show up with a raccoon in broad daylight in the middle of a crowded street, there will definitely be trouble. And not the kind either of us would enjoy. Besides, maybe I don't want another case right now. Honestly, I could really use a break."

"Level with me here. I'm going stir crazy. I've almost finished my second watch-through of all forty-ish seasons of Survivor. What am I supposed to do when I'm through with that, huh?"

"Start a third watch-through," I suggested with a shrug.

His jaw fell open as if I'd just made the most shocking and offensive recommendation of all time. It looked like he wanted to say something more, but before he could a car pulled onto our long driveway and began its approach to the house.

Pringle scurried off to hide, because as much as he liked bugging me and Nan, he was still wary of other humans. If he would have waited just a couple seconds longer, though, he would have seen that the new arrival was someone he'd come to trust, thanks to our recent adventures forcing them to work together while the rest of us were out of town.

"Hi, Charles," I said when my boyfriend parked and got out of his car. He wore his button-down shirt with the sleeves rolled up to the elbows and still wore his suit pants, although he'd ditched the jacket and tie.

"Ready to go?" he asked, waiting at the car door and eyeing me suspiciously.

I stood and brushed away the crumbs that had fallen to my lap while Octo-Cat and Pringle battled over the lobster roll.

"Angiiiie," Charles ground out. "Don't tell me you forgot!"

Somehow "forgot what?" didn't feel like the right response here, so I just smiled and batted my eyelashes.

"About the movie," he prompted. "It was your idea for us to see it tonight."

"Oh! Oh, right! I am so sorry, Charles. Things have just been..." I popped to my feet as I searched for the right word. Busy wasn't accurate, but I was still very overwhelmed, regardless. "They've been a lot lately. If you give me five minutes, I can run a brush through my hair and then we can go."

He shook his head and trotted up the steps,

taking me in his arms before I could slip away. "Let's stay in tonight," he said, pressing a soft kiss to my forehead and reminding me all over again why I was crazy about this particular man.

I looked up at him with half-lidded eyes. "You don't mind?"

"Nah." He pulled me to his chest and held me tight. "As long as I get to spend time with you, it doesn't really matter what we do. How about you choose tonight, and I'll choose what we do next time around."

We shared a slow kiss. I practically melted into him as he held me.

That is, until Octo-Cat rushed back through the pet flap and shouted, "Gaaah! You know I hate it when you two groom each other in my presence."

I laughed and kissed Charles again. Octo-Cat would just have to deal with it.

3

Charles and I ended up watching a made-for-TV movie on the Disney channel, which offered just the right amount of wholesomeness mixed with campiness to lighten my mood—and to send me drifting to sleep early.

The next morning, I woke up and took a quick shower, hoping it would help make me more alert for the day ahead. It didn't.

So I pulled on my favorite ratty polka-dot bathrobe and padded down to the kitchen, where I found Nan at the sink, rinsing some mixed berries in a colander.

"Good morning, sleepy head," she sang out. "I'll have you know, ten o'clock has already come and gone."

"Sorry," I said around a yawn. "I don't know why, but I've just been so exhausted lately."

Nan finished with the berries and patted her hands dry. "There's some vanilla yogurt in the fridge and granola in the cabinet, if you'd like to help yourself to a parfait."

"Right now I just need coffee," I mumbled, removing my French press from the dishwasher and setting to work. This was the latest in my attempts at satisfying my caffeine cravings without having to rely on an electric coffee maker. It took a bit more work, but I'd started to prefer the taste of the fresher brew that this process yielded.

"Any big plans for today?" I asked while I waited for the water to heat up.

Nan popped a particularly plump raspberry into her mouth and sighed with pleasure. "Grant and I are going to take the ferry out to Caraway Island and do some window shopping."

I'd never quite understood the older generation's obsession with window shopping. Was it really shopping if you went knowing you wouldn't be buying anything? I was pretty frugal with my money, but even I couldn't see the appeal of that activity.

"Sounds like a nice, relaxing day," I said with my lips pressed into a tight smile.

"Oh, my dear grandchild, it's boring, and you know it." Nan winked at me, and we both giggled.

"Then why are you doing it?"

"That's how love works sometimes, sweetie. I agree to one of Grant's activities knowing that next time I'll get to make the plans for the day."

Nan and Mr. Gable, the owner of the local jewelry shop and head of the downtown commerce committee, had been dating since the holidays, and they made the sweetest couple, too.

Nan's chihuahua Paisley had recently become good friends with Grant's rabbit, E.B.—short for Easter Bunny. At first the little thing was terrified of our pets, but even she could see that sweet Paisley would never harm a soul. Octo-Cat, on the other hand, give him opposable thumbs and he would have gladly used them to assist in making rabbit stew.

"Charles said something like that last night, too," I mumbled, searching through the cupboards to select a coffee mug. Call me superstitious, but I tended to believe that the choice of coffee cup could impact one's entire day. I bypassed the #1 Private

Investigator mug Charles had gifted me for Valentine's Day in favor of a fun color-changing mug inspired by one of my favorite book series. Every time I used it, I made another solemn promise that I would be up to no good. And that always made me smile.

I took a slow glorious sip of mid-morning bliss just as a knock sounded on the front door. I turned to Nan, but she simply shrugged and returned to fiddling with the berries.

So I went to answer the door, bleary-eyed, in a ratty bathrobe, and with zero percent blood-coffee ratio.

And there on the other side of the door stood Charles, wearing cargo khaki shorts and a fitted T-shirt with sports sunglasses pushed up into his hair. Honestly, I hardly recognized him outside of his usual monkey suit.

He glanced over my shoulder with his brows pinched together. "Didn't you tell her?"

"No," Nan answered. I hadn't even heard her creep up behind me. "You said you wanted it to be a surprise. I'll go grab her bag for you."

"What's going on?" I asked, turning to look from Charles to my grandmother, hoping that one might provide me with an explanation.

Nan walked away, raising a hand over her shoulder as she went.

I turned back toward my boyfriend, who stared at me with wide eyes and an even wider smile. "We're going on a surprise getaway," he announced, grabbing my hands and giving them a good squeeze.

"But I just got back from getting away," I said with a frown. I hated to be a downer; however, my last vacation was anything but relaxing. Between driving cross-country, winding up in a car accident, and finding out Nan had been blabbing my secrets to anyone who would listen, I was just plain exhausted.

"This time it will be just you and me going out for a long and quiet weekend," he explained, before leaning into whisper, "No pets."

This drew a happy sigh from me. I loved my animals dearly, but I could never fully relax in their presence knowing I had to work hard at not exposing my secret in front of the wrong person. Even though they knew very well that I couldn't talk to them in front of people who didn't already know about my ability, that didn't stop them from chattering on and filling my head with constant noise. The worst part was when I had to try to follow two separate lines of conversation. It made my brain tired.

A weekend away could be just the trick

Nan returned rolling a wheeled suitcase behind her. "All packed and ready to go. I just need another five minutes to finish packing the picnic." She left the luggage with us and hurried back to the kitchen.

"Where are we going?" I asked, starting to get a little excited.

Charles pressed his lips into a firm line and shook his head. "It's a surprise."

"But there will be a picnic?" I prompted, tilting my head as I studied his face for hints. "Does that mean we're going somewhere outside?"

He drew his thumb and forefinger across his mouth. "Not telling. You'll see when we get there."

I raised an eyebrow. "What about work?"

"The firm can keep things together for one day without me. I don't think I've ever used a full vacation day. It was time. And besides, I may have snuck into the office early to get a few things taken care of before coming here."

"Ah-ha. I knew it!"

Charles laughed. "Yeah, we both need this break."

Nan returned with a cute woven basket in hand and gave it to Charles.

"Thanks," he said with a big grin. "And you're sure you're okay to look after Jacques and Jillianne while we're away?"

Last year, Charles had taken in my former neighbor's two Sphynx cats after her untimely demise. They had never much warmed up to me, and I doubted they liked Nan, either. Still, Charles had grown quite fond of his two hairless babies.

Nan nodded vigorously and pushed us toward the door. "I've got it all under control. Paisley and I will go pay them a visit later this afternoon. Now get out of here. Go have some fun. Goodness knows you two both need it!"

Well, she was right about that, I supposed.

I just hoped whatever Charles had planned for us would be every bit as relaxing as he'd promised.

And that Octo-Cat wouldn't be too mad at me for abandoning him this weekend.

4

Outside, a massive white vehicle sat waiting partway down our driveway.

"Surprise!" Charles shouted as he strode ahead of me with both the suitcase and picnic basket in tow.

I gasped and stopped in my tracks, blinking twice to make sure my eyes weren't misleading me. "You bought an RV?"

He turned back to smile at me before continuing on his way. "I didn't buy it. There's this new app that's kind of like Airbnb meets Uber. So I rented this baby from someone over in Cooper's Cove. It's ours through Monday. Your Nan's already agreed to return it for me, too."

I jogged to catch up. "There's no way you're

letting Nan drive this. That woman is a terror on wheels, and you know it."

Charles just laughed and opened the passenger door for me. "Climb on up. We've got about three hours to get to our destination, so not too bad."

"Climb on up?" I repeated. "I'm in my ratty bathrobe. I'm not going anywhere until I get changed."

"No, that's why I had Nan pack you a bag. You can get changed on the way."

"That's ridiculous. We're right here. I'm going to go inside and change and then we can get going."

Before he could drag me into the RV, I turned and climbed the porch and pulled on the door. Locked.

"Really, Nan?" I shouted at the locked door. "You're sending me off in just a bathrobe?"

"Don't worry, I packed you something nice," she shouted back through the door.

It was obvious that these plans were in motion and there was nothing I could do to stop this runaway camper. With a sigh, I wrapped my robe tighter around myself and walked back over to the RV.

I hoisted myself inside while Charles went around back to the living area where he stashed my suitcase and the picnic basket. Rather than buck-ling up, I spun in my seat to check out our hotel on wheels. It had a small kitchen area complete with linoleum floor and a sink, cute little stovetop, and a half-sized fridge. Across from that sat a comfy-looking booth and table flanked by a built-in couch. Further back, I could just glimpse a bedroom with dark drapes and what appeared to be a queen-sized bed—whatever the size, it definitely took up a good deal of space.

Charles swung himself up onto the driver's seat. "There's a bathroom back there if you need it, and I've stocked up on food for the weekend, too."

"Seems like you've thought of everything," I said as I settled into my seat and drew the safety belt across my lap.

"Nan and I planned the whole thing together last night while you dozed on the couch," he admitted with a sheepish grin.

"If you would have told me, I could have—"

"If I would have told you, you'd have found a reason not to go," Charles interrupted, which was fine. I hadn't really known where I was going with that statement, anyway.

"Fair, but you realize Nan could have packed my suitcase with nothing but evening gowns or pajama bottoms with silk blouses, or only old Halloween costumes."

A look of mock horror flashed across Charles's face, but then he shook his head and turned on the mega-watt smile again. "Nah, she knew where we were headed."

"Since when has that mattered to my nan?" I asked with an admittedly nervous laugh as Charles turned the key over in the ignition and slowly navigated the camper down the rest of the driveway.

"Not knowing what to expect is part of the fun. Right?" He stopped and shot me a quick glance before pulling carefully out onto the main road.

"Oh, I know exactly what to expect," I countered. "Complete and utter chaos. You know, you could have at least let me change out of my bathrobe before we left."

Charles tapped his bare wrist while keeping his eyes fixed on the road ahead. "We have a very tight schedule to keep."

I tilted my head to the side and considered this. "But I thought this weekend was all about relaxing?"

"It is. Just within the parameters of our schedule. Besides, I have something special planned for later."

"I don't suppose you're going to tell me what that is."

"Oh, my sweet, sweet Angie, why won't you let me surprise you every once in a while? It's part of the fun in being your boyfriend, getting to spoil you when you least expect it."

"I've dealt with too many murders, kidnappings, and thefts to ever fully let my guard down," I admitted, then chewed on my lip as a fresh wave of anxiety washed over me.

Charles either didn't notice my uncertainty or didn't mind. "And that's precisely why we need this weekend away," he said. "Now sit back and relax. Here, this should help."

He plugged his phone into the vehicle's dash with a USB cable, then turned the radio on. Immediately upbeat percussion mixed with the cheerful tune of a whistle. I couldn't help but roll my eyes.

"Bob Marley?" I asked with a laugh.

"It's your Don't Worry, Be Happy mix. Made sense to kick it off with the title jam. Now seriously, it's time for you to chillax." He was so cute when he tried to use slang. Not only was his vocab severely outdated, it was also from the wrong region. He'd grown up in California, which was just about as far from Maine as one could get.

"And I suppose Nan helped you with this, too?"

"Let's just say there's more Sinatra than I might have otherwise chosen."

"Not necessarily a bad thing," I said, then held my hand over my mouth in a weak attempt to hide the yawn that followed.

"See, your body wants to chillax. Let your mind follow," Charles said in a woo-woo voice like the people at the massage place in Dewdrop Springs liked to affect.

"Yeah, I'm wicked tired," I said, eliciting a groan from Charles. He'd once told me that no matter how long he lived in Blueberry Bay, he would never ever use the term "wicked" to refer to anything other than a warty green witch.

I smiled at the memory, then closed my eyes. I must have nodded off, because the next thing I knew, a sudden crash in the back of the RV startled me awake.

"What was that?" I shouted, jumping in my seat, only to be forced back down when the seatbelt jerked tight against my chest. It took me a moment to remember where I was and why.

"We're almost there, but I'll pull over at the next exit so we can investigate," Charles said from beside me.

I shook my head. "No, don't do that. I can go check it out."

Before he had the chance to argue, I unbuckled my seatbelt and stood on shaky feet, keeping my hands out to either side for balance. It took me a moment to locate the source of the crash, mostly because everything looked exactly the same as it had when I'd first taken stock of the living space.

I carefully made my way through the kitchen and dining space and back to the bedroom, but it was completely undisturbed.

At last, I yanked open the door to the tiny bathroom and discovered exactly what I'd been searching for. Assorted toiletries covered the floor and the handheld shower head had come loose and was dangling toward the ground.

"Everything okay back there?" Charles called.

"Yeah. Just some stuff that fell over in the bathroom," I yelled back.

"Ouch, my ears," came a familiar voice, one I definitely hadn't expected to hear in that moment.

I followed the sound and spotted Pringle sitting on the floor beside the toilet. "Pringle, what are you doing here?" I shouted in disbelief. He was the very last creature I needed along for my relaxing weekend.

"We stowed away," the raccoon announced with a smile on his snout.

Horror knotted in my gut. "We?"

"Why didn't you let us out of here sooner? It's not at all comfortable in this cramped little bathroom," Octo-Cat whined, emerging from the narrow cabinet beneath the sink.

I balked. "Seriously, you're mad at me right now? You're not even supposed to be here!"

"We figured it was an oversight that you didn't invite us, so we invited ourselves," the irksome trash panda said matter-of-factly.

Blood flew through my veins and my heart whomped at an accelerated pace. "How?" I managed through gritted teeth.

Pringle pointed toward the ceiling, drawing my eyes to an air vent that sat propped open, providing more than enough space for two mischievous creatures to climb inside.

"Charles," I called, still staring at the open hatch above. "We have a bit of a problem back here!"

5

By the time Charles and I discovered our two furry stowaways we were less than a half hour from our destination, which put us in quite the pickle.

"Obviously we have to take them back," I tried to reason.

But he insisted that we stick to the schedule he'd already laid out, which meant we didn't have the time to add a five-hour delay by circling back home to drop off Pringle and Octo-Cat.

"It will be fine," he promised, even though I could tell that he, too, was unhappy about this particular turn of events. "They can hang back in the RV while we go do other things," he added, then turned up the volume on our no-worries playlist.

Frankly, I had lots of worries, but there was no point in hashing them out over and over again. Like Charles, I would just have to sweep my troubles to the back corner of my mind and do my best to have a good time.

We only had time to listen to a few more songs before we pulled into a little campground near the base of Mount Katahdin.

"Surprise!" Charles cried as he navigated to an open lot. Of course, I'd already figured out our destination a long time back but hadn't let on.

"Mount Katahdin, the tallest mountain in the entire state. It's supposed to be really beautiful here," he continued. "The perfect place to kick back and relax, starting with a hike! After all, the name literally means, 'The Greatest.'"

Hiking up a mountain was definitely not what I considered R&R, but at least I could be certain our furry stowaways wouldn't try to follow us there.

Charles leaned over to give me a peck on the cheek. "You go get changed, and I'll check in with the owner of the campgrounds to let her know we're here." He clambered up from the driver's seat and almost skipped out the door, leaving me with the unenviable task of trying to find appropriate attire in a bag packed by my crazy nan.

I padded back to the bedroom where my suitcase sat waiting for me on a bed made with perfect,
tight hospital corners. Octo-Cat and Pringle lay
stretched out on either side of it, both dozing away
as if they hadn't a care in the world.

I clapped my hands together as loud as I could,
startling them both awake. "Out," I said when they
turned their heads to me.

"You're disturbing our nap," Octo-Cat droned.

"And you're disturbing my vacation," I shot
back.

"Do what you need to do," Pringle said while
Octo-Cat stood and turned in slow circles, padding
at the bed.

I'd changed in front of my cat hundreds of
times, but I didn't feel comfortable getting
undressed in front of the raccoon. Privacy was
tricky business when it came to talking animals. Of
course they didn't view things the same way
humans did, but the ever-observant Pringle could
easily spot a weird mole or birthmark and then find
a way to bring it up in every single conversation we
had from that point on. I, for one, refused to give
him that kind of power over me.

"Out," I repeated, stamping my foot for good
measure. When Pringle still didn't budge, I took off

my bathrobe and threw it over him, then picked up the bundle and set it outside the door, which I shut firmly behind me.

"Your pajamas don't match," Octo-Cat said. And because nothing could ever be easy, he'd now settled himself on top of my suitcase.

I picked him up and sat him back on the bed. He wasn't happy about it, but at least I could trust him not to bite me.

Taking a deep breath in, I unzipped the suitcase, preparing for the worst assortment of clothes I'd long since relegated to the back of my closet. I hadn't, however, prepared myself to find a bag filled with outfits that weren't even mine.

I snapped a quick picture and fired off a text to Nan: Explain.

My phone rang a few seconds later. I picked up, and Nan's words rushed out. "I had to keep it a surprise, and you were in your room right up until go time. I had no other options, so I did the best I could."

"You do realize we don't wear the same size?" I said, eyeing the suitcase warily.

"That's why I picked stretchy things. Relax, you're going to look fabulous!"

I let out a long sigh. At this point, I was getting

very sick of everyone telling me to relax. "Okay. By the way, Octo-Cat is with me. Long story. Tell ya later. Gotta go," I muttered before ending the call.

After rummaging through the bag, I found there were two choices here. I could choose from a couple different floor-length, form-fitting gowns, or I could wear Nan's hot pink sweats with the word "juicy" written across the tush.

"Kill me now," I moaned as I cycled through my options again and again, trying to pick the lesser evil.

"Ask me later after I've had my nap," my cat answered unhelpfully.

In the end, I chose the juicy track suit, opting to keep my pajama T-shirt on top so that I could tie the jacket around my waist and hide the branded booty.

I'd just finished pulling my hair into a high and tight ponytail when a knock sounded on the door. "Ready to hit the trail?" Charles called.

"Ready." I opened the door, and he grinned, handing me a bottle of water.

"Looking good." He winked and he motioned for me to lead the way out of the RV.

I exited into the bright sun, wishing I'd had the foresight to grab some sunglasses on my way out of the house. I hadn't been awake enough yet to think properly then. I wasn't even sure I was awake enough now.

Charles exited the RV after me with a picnic basket slung over his arm.

"Wouldn't a backpack be better?" I asked, pointing to the awkward cargo.

"We don't have that far to go. It's just a short walk to a nice clearing that overlooks the water." He locked the door and then shoved the keys in his pocket. "Don't you think I know better than to make you work out on your big day off?"

I smiled and leaned into his side, and he slung an arm over my shoulders.

Perhaps this wouldn't be such a terrible trip after all.

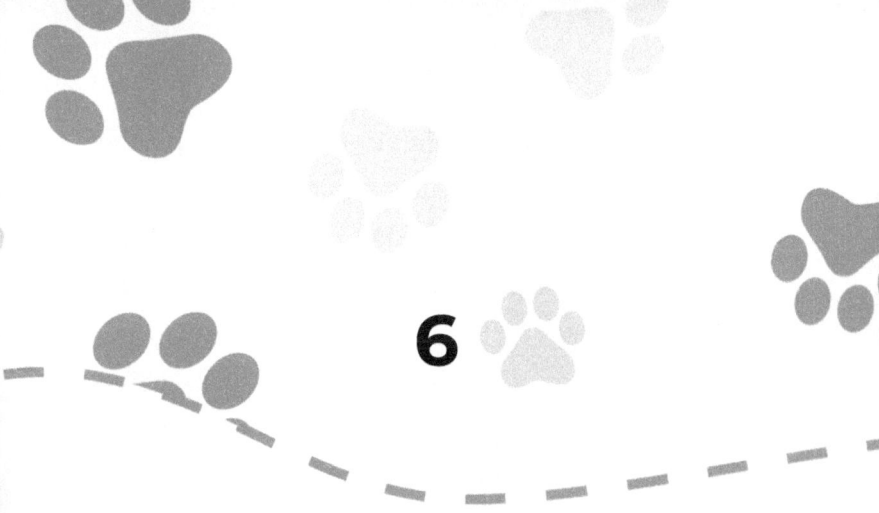

6

Charles and I walked hand in hand to the spot he'd pre-selected for our picnic, and it was every bit as lovely as promised.

It was still quite early in the season, but this was also the first nice weekend after a long and hard winter, which meant that campgrounds were packed. In fact, all of the tables that had been setup in the clearing were already filled with picnickers.

"C'mon," Charles said, tugging me along. "Let's find our own little spot off the beaten path.

Thankfully, the fresh air and beautiful scenery had already begun to do wonders for my sour mood. As we walked, I glanced back at the trail behind us a few times to make sure no uninvited animals had decided to join our trek, and each time I didn't spot them, my smile grew wider and wider.

And my fantastic boyfriend had planned an impromptu getaway because he knew that I needed it. How lucky was I?

We walked another five minutes until we came upon an enormous white ash tree. By the time we settled ourselves at its base, I was more than ready for the break—and the sustenance. I'd only managed half a mug of coffee that morning before our big adventure began and was looking forward to filling my stomach with the feast Nan had prepared. Yes, even though she was terrible at picking out clothes for me, Nan's cooking beat all.

"Let's see what we have here," Charles said, rubbing his hands together before lifting the lid on the basket. The scream that followed made us jump back in fight.

"What is it?" I asked with a gasp.

But Charles didn't answer. He simply pointed at the basket with a shaky finger.

Okay. I gulped and crawled forward on my hands and knees to see for myself.

I'm not proud to admit that I yelled out a string of curses at the top of my lungs when I discovered what was inside. Needless to say, there was no delicious picnic waiting for us. Instead I found one very fat and happy raccoon covered in sticky berry juice.

"Pringle!" I cried. "How could you?"

He flopped out of the basket and rolled right into me, splattering my borrowed hot pink sweats with deep red juice.

I groaned in frustration.

Pringle moaned in discomfort. "I was just going to nab a quick taste, but then I heard Charles coming, so I hid. I didn't know he'd take the basket with me in it. And then the two of you were walking and walking for what felt like forever, and I'm a nervous eater, so I decided to help myself to the rest of what you had in here."

"Why didn't you say anything?" I demanded, my brows pinched together in fury.

He rolled his eyes as if this whole thing was my fault and not his. "I just did."

"Before that, I mean."

The raccoon moaned again and clutched at his belly. "Everything was so good. I just couldn't stop." He rolled onto his side and studied me with dark, glistening eyes. "Say, do you think Nan will make me another of those strawberry cream cakes once we're back home? Because that was one of the best things I've ever tasted."

"I'll make sure she doesn't," I fumed. At least none of the other campers were around to see the crazy lady yelling at a raccoon.

"Now go wash yourself off in a creek or something. You look like you just walked out of a crime scene," I said with a scowl before relaying the whole thing to Charles.

As I talked, Pringle loped away. His entire coat was stained with berry juice, giving him a blood-soaked zombie roadkill appearance that made us both cringe.

"It's fine. Everything will be fine," Charles said with a smile that felt forced. "We'll relax here for a little bit before heading back. We can grab something for lunch once we're back at the RV."

"Yeah, if Octo-Cat hasn't already eaten it all." I crossed my arms over my chest and frowned. I didn't want to be a bummer, but I was just so, so disappointed, and I knew Charles was, too.

"We can still turn this weekend around," he promised as he leaned back against the thick tree trunk and pulled me to his chest. Then he repeated for the dozenth time, "I have it all planned out." It was quickly becoming his getaway mantra.

He then went on to tell me about his plans for

campfires and swimming and simply lounging about in the RV, enjoying each other's company. "We're skipping fishing, though. I figured with your ability, that would be kind of a nightmare scenario. Ah, please don't eat me!" he cried in a silly, high-pitched voice.

Honestly, I was already this close to becoming a vegetarian. The only thing that stopped me was that all my animal friends also ate meat, even though they could talk to each other, too.

"Are you ready to head back?" Charles asked after we'd sat snuggled up against that tree for a good twenty minutes.

I stretched my arms overhead, then let out a groan. "We can't leave without Pringle. He might not be able to find his way back."

Charles arched one eyebrow. "And that's a problem because?"

I shoved him playfully. "I know he can be a pest, but for better or worse, he's our pest."

"You won't be calling me a pest when you see the present I've brought you," Pringle called, emerging tail-first from the nearby brush.

Uh-oh. There's no way a present from Pringle could be a good thing.

A glint of silver caught my attention—the

sunlight reflecting off the scales of an enormous salmon that Pringle dragged behind him.

"How did you manage to get that?" I asked in surprise.

He paused to flash us a giant grin. "I felt bad about eating all your food, so I went and secured new food."

"And by secured you mean...?"

Pringle dragged the fish the rest of the way to us, then stood on his hind legs and admitted, "Okay, so I had a little help. Gloria, come on out!"

I followed his eyes as he turned back toward the brush, where a massive grizzly bear emerged.

Charles jumped to his feet and spread his arms to block me. "Angie, get down! Or run! I won't let him hurt you!"

I gulped hard, then rose to my feet and put a hand on my boyfriend's shoulder. "It's okay. I think the bear's friends with Pringle. Let me just talk to them before you freak out. Okay?"

I turned to Pringle so he could explain.

"Not a friend. A client," Pringle bit out the words, taking extra care to enunciate clearly. "Gloria's just brought us a new case, and she's already paid up front with this beauty." He motioned toward the fish. "Isn't that great?"

I could think of a lot of words to describe this situation, but not a single one of them was "great."

7

"What have you gotten us into?" I whispered to the raccoon, all the while hoping that bears had poor hearing. I'd never come across one face-to-face, so I honestly didn't know what to expect.

"Relax," Pringle said, holding his hands out in front of him. "She just needs a small favor. It's easy, I promise."

"We'll talk about this later," I said from the side of my mouth, then strode toward the bear with a tight-lipped smile. I didn't know enough about bears to determine whether showing my teeth would be construed as a threat, and with an animal as big and powerful as this one, I wasn't taking any chances.

"Hello," I called cheerfully, stopping several feet away. "Gloria, is it?"

The grizzly dipped her head in a nod. "Are you the Pet Whisperer P.I.?" she asked in a soft, feminine voice.

I hated the moniker that Nan and my mom had stuck me with. They thought it was a fun gimmick, but I thought it was way too close to revealing my secret. As it was, half the world thought I was crazy while the other fraction believed I really did have some kind of magical or psychic powers.

"I am," I answered, mimicking the bear's movement from before. "But I'm only here for the weekend. Can I help you with something before I go?"

Gloria padded forward on all fours, and it took everything I had not to flinch or back away from fright. "I won't hurt you," she said.

"I know. I'm sorry. It's just my first time meeting a bear."

She plopped into a sitting position and sighed. "That's the thing. Everyone assumes that bears are so scary, but really it's us that are afraid of you."

I raised a finger and pressed it into my chest. "Me? You're afraid of me?"

She nodded. "You seem like a nice enough

human, but so many others..." Her words faded away, and a shiver wracked her enormous body.

We looked at each other without saying anything.

Pringle hung back with his fish, but Charles crept forward and stopped at my side, threading his fingers through mine and giving my hand a good squeeze.

"Is this your mate?" Gloria asked, studying him with wide eyes.

"He is," I answered decisively. Charles and I weren't married—or even engaged—but animals tended to commit to each other very early on in their acquaintanceships. In the animal kingdom, Charles and I were basically like an old, married couple at this point.

"He protects you. That's good." Gloria gave an approving nod, then redirected her gaze toward the ground. "My mate was not so kind. He was at first, but as soon as the cubs were born, he tried to kill them—his own children—and so I ran away with the cubs and ended up here. It's close enough to the humans that he won't attempt to follow us here. But being close to the humans has created other problems for our little family."

My heart went out to her. Of course, I would

help if I could. I wasn't even angry at Pringle anymore for bringing Gloria to meet me. Granted, I was still mad at him for half a dozen other things... but not this.

"How can I help?" I asked, suddenly viewing bears in a whole new light—or at least the female ones.

"We only woke up from hibernation a few days ago, but already we're having big problems. The people who come to this park wander too close to our den, and sometimes they bring loud, exploding lightning that makes the little ones quake with fear."

It took me a moment to realize she meant fireworks. No wonder she and the cubs were so afraid.

"I'm pretty sure people aren't allowed to bring those into the park."

"Well, they do."

"If it's already against the law, I'm not sure what I can do to make it stop."

Gloria glanced back over her shoulder as if searching for something. When she continued, her words came out much faster. "There's a woman who oversees the campgrounds. She's in charge of looking after the visitors. Maybe she doesn't realize what's going on or how distressing it is—not only to the bears, but to all wildlife that call this park home. Would you please talk with her on our behalf?"

"You want me to talk with her?" I asked, cocking my head to the side.

The she-bear nodded. "Be our voice."

"Okay, Gloria. I'd be happy to do that for you." I smiled, forgetting to keep my teeth concealed.

Gloria stumbled back, then caught herself. "Please promise me you'll do it soon. I'm not sure my cubs can take another sleepless night."

I bowed. "You have my word."

"When it's done, come back to this spot and call my name. I will bring you another salmon as thank you for your efforts on my family's behalf." She shifted back onto all fours, watching me closely.

I raised a hand in protest. "That's okay. You really don't—"

"I must. That way I'll also know when it is done. Thank you, kind human. You do the animals in this wood a great service." And with that, she turned and wandered back from whence she came.

Well, what was one more task before finally settling into our relaxing weekend? Ultimately, it wouldn't make much of a difference for me, but it could be a huge help to Gloria, her cubs, and the other animals who called the park home.

Charles squeezed my hand, and I turned into his chest. "Is everything okay?" he asked.

"Yes, we just have to make a quick pit stop before we can have lunch. C'mon."

8

Charles and I made quick work of the walk back to camp, mostly because my stomach was growling worse than a grizzly in distress. And now that I had an adequate frame of reference, I could totally make that comparison, thank you very much.

Pringle hitched a ride in the berry-stained picnic basket, which I carried while Charles handled the salmon. To prevent our little stowaway from getting dirty again, I padded the basket interior with Nan's track suit jacket. Of course, this meant that my juicy booty was now exposed to anyone who dared take a peek at my derriere.

And that wasn't the only thing I had to be embarrassed about in this campsite full of strangers. I also desperately clung to the hope that no one would ask us how we managed to catch this massive salmon without any fishing gear on us, because I had no idea what lie I could tell to get us out of that one.

That's how we returned to the RV park—a hidden raccoon, a berry-stained track suit, juicy booty, and big fish to boot. Understandably, a few people paused what they were doing to openly gawk at us. But mostly folks let us go about our business.

"That's her camper right there." Charles pointed with his chin as we approached an older model RV with an army of pink plastic flamingos forming a makeshift fence around the front.

He took the basket from me, struggling to hang on to both it and the fish.

Pringle chittered something as he got jostled around, but it was too muffled for me to make out his exact words. Also I didn't care. Frankly, the whole thing served him right.

"I'll see you back at ours," Charles said, dawdling off with a very awkward gait as he attempted to balance the salmon on top of the heavy raccoon basket. "Good luck. I know you'll do great!"

Well, at least one of us had confidence in me and my persuasive abilities.

I ran my hands over the front of my pants to wipe off the dark juice that had transferred from the basket onto my fingers, then walked past the tango line of flamingos and knocked on the door.

When no one answered, I knocked again.

"If she's not answering, feel free to go right in. Junetta has a door's always open policy for folks at the campground," someone called, then popped her head through the open window of an aqua-accented Airstream parked in the adjacent lot to the right. She brushed her also aqua-accented curls out of her face and studied me with casual interest before pulling her head back inside.

"Thank you!" I called after her, then pushed the door open and stepped inside the dimly lit interior.

This was not nearly as luxurious as the model that Charles had rented for our weekend away. For one, it looked like the darker side of my normal wardrobe. Not everything about the 80s was fun and brightly colored. Some parts were brown and orange with avocado-colored refrigerators. I even spied a bit of rust around the faucet of the sink in the kitchenette. It all sort of clashed with the happy kangaroo logo on the outside.

Never matter.

No judgment. That wasn't what I was here for. I was here to negotiate on behalf of the animals. I didn't know this person, so I had no idea what to expect. Still, the worse she could do was say "no" to what I asked. Part of me wondered what she'd say to Gloria if she could've asked for herself. I chuckled to myself a bit at the thought.

"Hello," I called as I tiptoed back toward the bedroom.

The door hung open just a crack—not enough for me to get a good look inside. Seeing as I didn't want to catch Junetta in a compromised position, I knocked gently.

The door creaked open a little more, and a familiar, rotten smell wafted out to assault my senses.

"Hello?" I asked again, begging my suspicions to be wrong.

When no one answered, I held my breath, covered my nose, and pushed the door open the rest of the way.

On the bed, an older woman with a wrinkled face and unnaturally curly, copper-colored hair lay splayed out. One hand clutched at her stomach while the other groped the comforter—or at least it had until all life had left it. The bed had been nicely made, but a portion of the blanket had since been pulled and twisted.

The scene showcased a jarring mix of chaos and slumber. Junetta had suffered, but now she lay still. The smell I'd detected came from a puddle of pink-tinged vomit that had seeped into the carpet in front of the bed.

I stepped back out, taking care to shut the door behind me and give the poor woman some semblance of privacy. Partly just to shut the smell out. My fingerprints were already on it, anyway.

As I carefully retraced my steps back through the main living space of the camper, I spotted a half-eaten slice of pie sitting on the table. The fork had fallen to the ground, while the remainder of the pie was nowhere to be seen. Provided it had even been in here at all.

I stepped toward the table and examined the dessert. Mixed berry. Judging from the scene in the bedroom, my best guess was that it was poisoned.

I had to tell somebody.

Tearing my eyes away from the murderous pie, I rushed back out the door and jogged right toward the Airstream where the woman had stuck her head through the window to urge me into Junetta's RV when she hadn't answered the door.

This time, I must have knocked with a bit too much vigor because when the woman pulled the door open, her eyes darted back and forth wildly, her large, cat-eyed glasses making her look more like an owl as she attempted to make sense of the scene.

"Sh-sh-she's dead," I sputtered, taking a step back and pointing toward the flamingo-adorned trailer.

"What?" The woman clambered down the steps and stood to face me outside. While she'd stood in the doorway, I hadn't realized just how tiny she was. If I had to guess, I'd say she barely cleared five feet.

I sucked in a deep breath and let it out again before I attempted to explain. "Junetta. She's dead. Someone poisoned her, I think."

She squinted her eyes at me as if gazing into the sun—and given the angle she had to tilt her face to meet my eyes, perhaps she was. "Who are you?"

"I'm Angie. My boyfriend and I just arrived today. I had to talk to her about some-thing, and you told me to go right in. When I did, I found her body in the bedroom."

She studied me for a good long moment without saying anything more. And even though I towered over her, and even with her resembling a lawn gnome from the 1950s, I still found her quite intimidating as she sized up me and my story.

Her eyes bore into mine as she announced, "I'm calling the cops." Then she hurried back into her Airstream, slamming the door straight in my face.

Well, that had not gone as planned. Nope, not at all.

9

returned to our RV to find Charles standing at the kitchenette with a spatula in hand.

"Hope you're in the mood for grilled cheese. It's the house, er rather, RV special today," he said, but then he caught the look on my face, set both the spatula and the fry pan aside, and came to meet me where I stood. "What's wrong? Did you talk to the camp manager? Was she not willing to help?"

I stared straight ahead, my head shaking and eyes unfocused, still recalling the horrible scene I had stumbled upon only moments before.

"Angie?" Charles prompted, placing a hand on my arm.

"She can't help," I whispered as I finally met his eyes. A shiver wracked through me. "She's dead."

"Who's dead?" Pringle chirruped from the front of the camper, bringing me back to the present moment. I craned my head and spotted him in the driver's seat where he stood gripping the steering wheel in his tiny hands, pretending to steer through traffic.

"Get back here," I demanded. "Those windows aren't tinted. Anyone could see you."

Thankfully, and rather uncharacteristically, he didn't argue. Which I was grateful for because I just didn't have the energy for it. It also told me I needed to be suspicious of the mischievous procyonid. But I also didn't have the energy to deal with the questions if another camper spotted him. Maine wasn't one of those crazy states where you could have a pet raccoon. We weren't like Delaware.

Pringle hopped down and then scampered over and hopped onto the couch. "Could, but didn't. Now what's your twenty, Mama Bear? I'm getting shutter trouble over here. Someone's dead? Who? Do we need to pull stakes and put the hammer down before this place is crawling with Smokies? Or do we have another case on our hands?"

I sank down into the booth seat, propped my

elbows on the table, and cradled my head in my hands. Pringle was exhausting at the best of times. Right now, though, it was like he was speaking another language.

"Sorry," Charles said as he slid onto the seat beside me and whispered, "He's been listening to the CB radio. Are you sure she's dead?"

"Positive."

"Do you need me to call the police or did you do that already?"

I shook my head and sighed. "I didn't have to. One of the other campers already did."

"Hey, that's good, right?" Leave it to my lawyer boyfriend to remain calm and log-ical, no matter the circumstance. I appreciated that about him, but right now I needed him to understand.

"No, it's not good at all. She called the police on me." My voice cracked at that last part. "She thinks I'm the one who killed her."

"Well, that's ridiculous. You haven't been out of my sight long enough to murder someone. Besides, who's to say she was even murdered?"

I lifted my head and stared at Charles with wide eyes. "I say she was murdered, Charles. Most likely with a poison pie. At least that's where the evidence is pointing."

His face fell and voice softened. "Oh, no. I'm sorry you had to see that."

"You'd think I'd be used to it by now with all the bodies I've managed to stumble upon lately."

"Well, I love you because you haven't gotten used to it." He kissed me on the forehead. "But you do seem to have some kind of gift for stumbling across bodies."

"Yeah, too bad I can't return it," I quipped. I went to drop my head back into my hands, but a blur of movement caught my eye.

Octo-Cat appeared bleary-eyed in the doorway to the bedroom. "Why so much noise? Some of us are trying to keep up with our beauty sleep. And aren't you all sup-posed to be out on a picnic?"

Pringle at least had the good sense to look embarrassed about the part he'd played in ruining this day. "10-44, good buddy. Smoke those brakes, it's a long story. And it ends with a Windy City rollover on our shoulder." When he was met with a sea of blank looks, Pringle brushed his face and added, "We've got dead body next door."

Octo-Cat reared back and hissed. "Angela! This is supposed to be a vacation. Heaven knows I've needed it. You're a lot to put up with even on your best days, I'll have you know. You can't just go around uncovering dead bodies while I'm trying to enjoy a long-overdue nap."

I groaned. "I didn't uncover the body on purpose, and I also never invited you to tag along. So no more complaints. I'm having a hard enough time dealing as it is."

Charles rubbed my back in big, sweeping circles. "Are they giving you a hard time?" he asked.

"They always give me a hard time," I moaned. This time we didn't even have sweet Paisley around to help keep spirits high. No, I was stuck with sassy and sassier.

"We should probably head out," Charles murmured. "When the police get here, they'll want to talk to you." He got up and moved back toward the kitchen, grabbing for the pan with the grilled cheese. Even off the heat for the length of time we'd been talking, one side was practically charcoal. He shook his head, then opened up one of the cabinets and took out a box. "You must be starving by now. Take this."

He handed me a Clif bar, and even though I had been famished not even ten minutes back, my appetite had now disappeared entirely.

"Thanks," I muttered anyway as I forced myself to stand.

"There are some folding chairs stashed in the cargo hold. I'll grab those and then meet you outside. And Angie?"

He waited for me to meet his eyes before continuing, "It's going to be all right."

All right, yeah. Everything would be fine.

It had to be, right?

I certainly hadn't murdered the campground manager. In fact, I didn't know a thing about her except that she could be a bit lax with the rules.

Still, I'd been under suspicion before. And for a lot less, too.

Now I couldn't dismiss the nagging feeling that things would get a lot worse be-fore they got any better.

10

"Let's get this convoy moving! Wait for me," Pringle shouted right before I closed the door to the RV.

Of course, I had to go back in to explain why I would not be waiting for him. "You have to stay inside," I said, hoping that would be enough.

He squinted his eyes and spoke in a husky voice not at all befitting of him. "But what if I have to pay the water bill?"

I blinked down at him in utter bewilderment. "What are you even talking about?"

"You know." The raccoon dropped his voice to a whisper. "The bathroom?"

"You're smart enough to use the toilet, aren't you?" I challenged with a smirk. "Either that or you can wait for dark and then sneak out to do your business then."

His shoulders slumped and he dropped down onto all fours. "Are you really going to make me hide out in this crummy camper the whole weekend?"

I glared down the bridge of my nose at him. "Yes, I really am. I would never have willingly brought you on this trip, but you took that choice away from me when you forced your way on board. The way I see it, you have no one to blame but yourself."

"Well, I am coming with you," Octo-Cat called from the kitchenette counter.

I glanced over and found him cleaning his face and paws after presumably licking all the butter off the unfinished side of the grilled cheese sandwiches.

"What? Why do you want to come?" I asked.

"Mostly because 'The Bandit' wants to but can't." The cat lifted his head and grinned at the raccoon. "But also because I'm your partner, and it sounds like we might have an investigation on our paws. I plan on claiming my share of our payment, so I might as well take on some of the work, too," he added, licking his chops with glee.

"Fair enough," I said, not bothering to tell him there wouldn't be any payment for this particular case.

"Not fair at all!" Pringle cried, throwing his body up against the door so we wouldn't exit without him.

Goodness gracious! Why did it feel like I was trying to deal with a couple of ornery toddlers here?

I shook my finger at him. "Listen up, good buddy. If I catch your big-rig raccoon butt outside of this camper even once, I'm demolishing your tree house, cancelling your cable TV, and throwing out the Nerf guns, too. Got it?"

He gulped hard. "N-n-not Carla. You wouldn't." Yes, the silly trash panda loved his Nerf gun so much, he'd named the darn thing.

I narrowed my gaze. "Care to try me? You know, I also think I heard Nan talking about a beagle at the shelter that needed a new home. Maybe you'd like a new play-mate?"

"You'll pay for this," the raccoon muttered as he stepped back from the door and disappeared into the bedroom.

"If I pay, you pay!" I shouted after him.

Octo-Cat chuckled as he leisurely made his way toward the door. "You sure told him."

"Don't think you're off the hook," I said, spinning toward the cat. "I'm still mad at you, too."

Octo-Cat gave his best approximation of a shrug. "You may be angry with me today, but I'm angry with you pretty much every day. As far as I see it, we're even for the time being," he said, sauntering over.

There was so much wrong with that statement, too much for me to even attempt to address. So instead of trying, I simply opened the door and motioned for my cat to walk out ahead of me.

Charles had grabbed a set of green fabric camping chairs and set them out in front of the RV.

The police had arrived as well. A cruiser sat parked at the edge of the campground, but the officers were nowhere to be seen. Probably already inside Junetta's home, taking stock of the scene.

A few other visitors to the campground had pulled out lawn chairs of their own and sat watching the scene unfold.

"Ugh, it smells bad," Octo-Cat said before unleashing a trio of mighty sneezes. "What is that strange yet alluring smell?"

"Charles..." I said, practically collapsing into the seat at his side. "Please let Octavius know that I'm not available to speak with him at the moment."

"Yeah, yeah, I get it," the tabby groaned. "Can't let these unimportant strangers know your big secret. Never mind that you'll probably never see any of them ever again. I'm sure they're all watching with rapt attention just in case they catch you talk-ing to a magnificent specimen of the feline species rather than—I don't know—gawking at the police investigation happening right under their noses. No, better you play it extra safe rather than actually discuss the case with your partner. Yeah, no thank you. While you sit here twiddling your thumbs, I'm going to investigate."

"No, bad kitty!" I called as he trotted away with his tail raised high and haughty. "Come back here right now!"

He'd almost made it to Junetta's trailer when a middle-aged woman with a blonde pixie cut and enough scarves to qualify as a makeshift kite stepped out from between two campers and scooped him into her arms.

"Where are you going, Mr. Tabby? You look way too fat and happy to be a stray. Maybe I should call you Mr. Tubby?" She stopped to laugh at her own joke. "You don't want your mommy worrying about you, do you? What do you say we go find her together?"

"I've never been so insulted in all my life," Octo-Cat yowled and attempted to squirm out of her arms.

"Now, now, Mr. Tubby-Tabby," the woman said. "I'm just trying to help you."

"I don't need your help," he growled as his wide amber eyes scanned the area in a panic. When he spotted me standing at the RV and attempting not to laugh, he shouted, "Angela! Help me!"

"He does not look happy," Charles said. "Are you going to go claim him?"

"In a second," I said, watching Octo-Cat's pupils grow wide with terror.

The blonde woman caught me watching her and called out, "Does this chubby little guy belong to you?"

"Again with the insults!" Octo-Cat hissed. "Bah!"

"Yes, he's mine. Thanks for grabbing him," I said, then silently added, *and for teaching him a bit of a lesson.*

"'ll go grab another chair," Charles said as the woman carrying Octo-Cat made her way over.

"Is that your husband?" she asked, watching Charles with a little too much interest as he left. "Because, if so... Well done, sister."

"My boyfriend," I corrected with an awkward smile. "And that's my cat."

"Lucky lady on both counts." The woman said plopped down into Charles's vacated seat while keeping a firm grip on Octo-Cat.

"My name's Angie," I offered.

"Sharon. Ahh!" Suddenly, she pulled her hand toward her face, showing off a bright scarlet scratch that now marred her pale skin.

Octo-Cat shouted a string of kitty curses and ran off to hide somewhere.

Sharon popped out of her chair to follow him, but I called her off. "Don't worry about him. He always comes back."

She clucked her tongue and settled back in the chair. "My Chester could sure take a lesson or two from him. What's your little tubster's name?"

From a distance, Octo-Cat yowled and spat even more insults at the woman. De-spite my irritation, even I was starting to feel a little bad for him.

"His name is Octo-Cat, and the vet says he's in the healthy weight range for his size. He's actually part Maine Coon on his grandmother's side." At least he always said that about his lineage. I had doubts about its veracity, though. It also wasn't exactly what the vet had said during our last visit. Octo-Cat had, in fact, crept a little above the recom-mended weight range—thanks, lobster rolls—but I had chosen not to share that particular tidbit with him.

Sharon shrugged and leaned back in the chair, stretching her legs straight out in front of her. "My Chessy just loves the RV life, even though he never leaves our little home on wheels. Why, I imagine he's enjoying himself a little nap in a sunbeam right about now."

Hmm. A regular. Perhaps she knew a thing or two about who might want Junetta dead.

"Do you and Chester come here often?" I asked conversationally.

Sharon laughed so hard she began to cough, then formed a fist and punched her chest several times. "Whoo! It's been a long time since I heard a pickup line."

My eyes widened. "I didn't mean—"

"Now don't you go taking it back. Just let me enjoy it." She let out a happy sigh, then sat silent for a few moments before speaking again. "Chester and I have a nice little rotation, and Katahdin is part of it. Each month we hit several of our favorite parks so that we can see all our friends across the state. Of course, most folks stay put during the winter months. But not Chester and me. We're always on the move. We're like sharks. If we stop swimming, we die." She laughed again, but not hard enough to send herself into another fit.

Throughout my life, I'd met few people who could talk as much as Sharon did—or with as little input from a conversational partner. So, yes, if I asked the right questions, I might be able to sneak a little of the local park gossip out of her.

"Did you notice the police car when it pulled up?" I asked, nodding toward the parked cruiser.

"Oh, yes. I most assuredly did. A couple of officers got out and marched right over to Junetta's. Between you and me, that woman is always in some kind of trouble. She had a nasty divorce last year. That's why she gave everything up and moved into the park permanently. Of course, that snake of an ex of hers shows up every so often begging her to take him back."

My features pinched in sympathy. "I had no idea."

"Well, why would you? You're a first-time visitor, right?" She bobbed her head and grinned. "I always recognize a first-timer."

I nodded, even though it seemed Sharon didn't need any confirmation from me.

At the same time, Charles returned with empty hands. "Couldn't find another chair, but I don't mind getting a little dirty," he announced before settling himself on the ground.

"Oh, I bet you don't." Sharon growled flirtatiously.

Charles's cheeks turned beet red.

"Well, I best get back to Chester. Say, why don't the two of you and Octo-Cat stop by mine later for coffee and gossip. What was your name again, dear?"

"Angie. And this is Charles." Of course, she remembered the cat's name, but not mine.

"Yes, definitely bring him along." Sharon puckered her lips and made a smooch-ing sound, then burst out laughing yet again.

"Well, as Tigger says, TTFN!" she sang, blowing us both kisses as she left.

"Wow," Charles said when the two of us were alone again. He got up from the grass and settled himself in the chair Sharon had just vacated.

"Yeah," I agreed, then hung my head back and watched the clouds as they idled by.

Finally, a moment of peace.

Of course, it didn't last anywhere near long enough.

"Over there! That's her!" a familiar voice shouted.

When I lowered my gaze, I saw the woman from the Airstream marching straight at us with a police officer following hot on her heels.

12

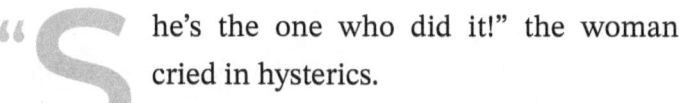

"She's the one who did it!" the woman cried in hysterics.

I rose from my chair, and Charles did the same. "I'm the one who discovered the body," I admitted.

"She's guilty!" the woman shouted again even though we were only standing a few feet apart.

"Ma'am," the officer said in a stern voice. "I'm going to have to ask you to give us some privacy."

He then turned toward me. "Mind if we talk inside?"

Unfortunately "inside" was something of a problem. That's where we had a rogue raccoon acting like a toddler while pretending to be a big-rig trucker.

I couldn't exactly refuse a request from the police, and the longer I hesitated, the more suspicious we would appear.

I shot a glance to Charles, who met my gaze with a subtle nod.

Charles strode up to the door and pushed it open.

I whispered a quick prayer under my breath as the policeman and I followed him inside.

"Is everything all right, miss?" the officer asked, catching me as I frantically searched the camper's living space.

No Pringle, which meant he was either hidden out of sight, or he'd snuck away despite my orders to remain put.

"I'm fine," I answered, perhaps a bit too tersely.

Charles motioned toward the table that was flanked with booth seats. "She's still in shock after that discovery. Please, won't you come sit?"

He studied Charles with fresh interest. "Were you with her when she discovered the body?"

"No, but I'm Miss Russo's attorney," he answered glibly.

Now the officer turned back to me. "You sure lawyered up quick for someone that—"

"She's also my girlfriend," Charles added before

the officer could take that any further. "We came up here for a relaxing getaway."

The policeman slid into one side of the booth, and I took the other. Charles sat beside me and held my hand under the table. The officer eyed us both for moment before pulling out his notepad and beginning.

"Ms. Stevens out there seems pretty convinced you're the one who killed our victim," the policeman said slowly, keeping a careful watch on my reaction.

It took everything I had to remain calm. Yes, I'd been suspected of murder before, but that was on my home turf. Here, I knew no one, and no one knew me.

"She's wrong." I pressed my free hand flat on the table. "I'm just the one who had the bad luck of discovering—"

"And why is that?" the officer interrupted, clicking his pen. "Why were you in her trailer uninvited?"

"She was the one who—" I spat, but Charles raised a hand to stop me.

"Angie was urged to enter the premises when her knocks went unanswered. Ms. Stevens herself was the one who told her to proceed."

"She said Junetta had an open-door policy," I added in a whisper.

The policeman tapped his pen on his notebook for a few beats. "What did you need to see her about?"

"My client is not under suspicion. Is she?" Charles asked, flipping into full lawyer mode. He moved his eyes from the officer's face down to the shiny badge on his shirt. "Officer Hamil, is it?"

"Yes, that's my name. And we're just gathering information right now," he replied before getting up to wander the tight living space.

He stopped at the kitchenette. "Burnt grilled cheese sandwiches. Are you usually such a disaster in the kitchen, Ms. Russo? Perhaps you're better at baking? Like, say, a pie?"

I gritted my teeth. Officer Hamil was clearly trying to rile me up. I knew that, and yet I had a hard time letting his rude and sexist remarks slide.

Charles squeezed my hand as a reminder that he was there for me, that he would make sure I came through this all right. "I was the one cooking lunch. Understandably, I stopped when Angie returned to the trailer and told me what she'd found."

"Boyfriend, lawyer, and personal chef," Hamil

said to me with a wink. "Is there any-thing this guy doesn't do?"

"He doesn't accuse innocent people of murder," I shot back before Charles could remind me to keep mum.

The policeman tilted his head to the side and opened his mouth without speak-ing. Was it really so hard to believe that someone would talk back to him in the same manner in which he spoke to others? "Now you wait just a min—"

A knock on the door cut him off.

"Mind if I answer?" he asked me, choosing to ignore Charles completely. Apparently he thought he had a better chance of getting a confession if he dealt directly with me. Too bad I wouldn't be confessing to a crime I'd had zero involvement in.

"Go right ahead," I said without missing a beat.

Officer Hamil kept his eyes on us for another few moments before sighing and heading toward the door.

"Yeah, what have you got?" he mumbled to whoever was there.

I strained to see, but his wide body blocked my view.

After a couple minutes of hushed conversation, he stepped back into the trailer and walked up to the table, standing close to Charles and blocking him in as some kind of intimidation technique.

"Not just a lawyer, chef, boyfriend, but also a convicted felon, eh?" He paused and sucked air through his teeth. "Sir, I'm going to ask you to come with me."

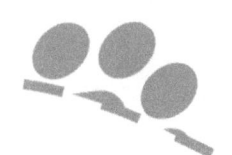

13

I tried to follow, but Officer Hamil wouldn't allow me to exit the vehicle.

"We'll just be a moment," he said before shutting the door firmly behind them.

Shoot. As much as I hated being the one under suspicion, I liked it even less when Charles came under fire. But the investigation wasn't my only problem.

"Pringle?" I whispered, still unsure where the nosy critter had gone.

When he didn't answer, I moved to the front of the RV and lowered the window a crack. Thankfully, it was just enough to listen to the conversation outside if I strained.

Officer Hamil was now joined by a female speaker. I didn't recognize her voice as belonging to the Airstream lady—Ms. Stevens—who was so completely and totally convinced that I had offed a woman I'd never even met.

This left me to assume that the woman in question was the other police officer who had arrived on the scene.

"This isn't my RV," Charles explained calmly.

"Stole it, did you?" Hamil asked, but the other officer shushed him.

"If it's not yours, then why is it in your possession?" she pressed. Already I liked her a lot better than her partner.

"Do you mind if I reach into my right front pocket to get my phone?" Bless him, Charles always knew exactly how to act in these situations.

"Go ahead," the woman said. I imagined her nodding, even though I hadn't the slightest idea what she even looked like.

"I'm watching you, lover boy," Hamil growled.

His partner shushed him again, then everyone fell silent as they waited for Charles to bring up what he wanted to show them.

"See," Charles said a short bit later. "This app

lets you borrow campers and camp equipment short-term. It's a bit like Airbnb. If you click here, you'll see the booking I made with the owner."

"That's the name that comes up for the plates," the lady cop said.

"That doesn't mean you're in the clear, though. Hand over your ID." Hamil was quick to take back control. It must have been awful having that blowhard as a partner.

"I'm going to reach into my back pocket now," Charles enunciated clearly.

"Hamil, why don't you run a scan while I take over here?" the woman officer suggested in a way that said compliance was non-optional.

Nobody said anything for a moment, and then the back door to our RV swung open.

I stayed where I was in that big bucket seat, mostly because I didn't want to get caught eavesdropping.

"Thanks, Officer Lenard," Charles said, his deep voice filling the space.

"You don't look like the aggravated assault type," she said kindly. "But just because I don't believe you committed this murder doesn't mean I don't want to talk to you."

"Understood. How can I help?"

The squeaking of leather signaled that they had slid into the booth.

"Walk me through your day," Lenard instructed after taking a moment to get settled. "Take extra care to mention any contact you had with the deceased."

"Well, this morning I woke up early to get some work in before picking up the camper, picking up my girlfriend, and hitting the road."

"Fast-forward to your arrival, please." Lenard would have made a good lawyer if she hadn't chosen to pursue law enforcement instead. She and Charles had the exact same way of being assertive while also remaining kind and professional.

"It was about a three-hour drive," he explained. "We arrived a little before two. I went to check in with the camp manager before taking my girlfriend to a picnic area a short walk away."

"You checked in with the camp manager? Tell me more about that."

"There's not much to tell. She came to the door when I knocked, but didn't invite me in. When I told her who I was so she could confirm my appointment, she asked me to wait and went back inside. She emerged a couple minutes later with a big logbook in hand and marked off my name. She said to stop on by if I needed anything during my stay, and that was it."

"Did you notice anything unusual during your interaction with her?" Officer Lenard pressed, her voice smooth and practiced. She'd likely questioned witnesses hundreds of times before. I imagined her as an older lady. Maybe a few years off from retirement, if she played her cards right.

"Just that she seemed distracted," Charles said. "But since I'd never met her before, I couldn't speak to whether or not that was normal behavior on her part."

"Understood, understood." They sat in silence for a few beats before Lenard spoke again. "So just to confirm, it was about two o'clock when you went to check in?"

"Yes."

"And your girlfriend discovered the body. What time was that?"

"Well, we left a few minutes after I checked in and walked about fifteen minutes to the picnic area. All the tables there were filled so we walked another five. We sat and relaxed for close to half an hour and then walked back. As soon as we arrived back at the campground, my girlfriend went to speak with the manager. I'd say that puts us at about three thirty this afternoon."

"Which gives us an hour and a half window for the death," Officer Lenard supplied. "What made your girlfriend so eager to check in, if you'd already done so?"

Oh, no. That question would have totally made me freeze up. If Charles explained what we'd really been doing—making business deals with bears—he'd instantly move up the suspect list.

"We thought we heard fireworks while we were out there," he explained, then stopped and sighed. "As an animal lover, she was quite distressed to think that something like that could be happening in a protected nature park."

Charles's reply came out so smooth and convincing that even I believed it. Well, the best lies were based on truth, and this was as close as we could come to sharing the conversation I'd had with Gloria at Pringle's behest.

"Are you certain you...?" I didn't hear the rest of the officer's response because something else caught my focus.

Pringle.

Straight ahead on the roof of the camper parked

in front of us. But before I could say or do anything, he dropped through the vent and disappeared from view.

Oh, he'd be in big trouble once I caught up to him!

14

I opened the passenger side door just as quietly as I could and slipped outside while Charles and Officer Lenard continued to converse inside.

I crept over to the RV where I'd seen Pringle sneaking about on the roof, all the while trying to figure out what I would say to explain myself to whoever was inside.

But when I knocked, nobody answered—an unfortunate theme of the day.

"Pringle!" I whisper-yelled. "Pringle! I know you're in there!"

"I think I have some Pringles back at mine if you've got a craving," Sharon yelled from somewhere behind me.

I jumped and did an about-face. "Oh, Sharon. Hi, again!" I cried, wiggling my fingers in her direction. "I was just searching for my cat."

She squinted at me in confusion. "I thought his name was Octo-Cat?"

"Oh, yes. Yes, it is. Pringle is his middle name. Well, one of them, anyway. His full name is Octavius Pringle Maxwell Ricardo Edmund Frederick Fulton Russo, Esq, P.I. See, that's why I had to shorten it. He comes to all the names, though, and since I haven't seen him for a while, I'm running through the list." I let out a nervous laugh. She was going to see right through me on this one.

But I got lucky.

"Tubby Tabby is missing?" Sharon shrieked, fanning herself with one hand. "Well, why didn't you come and get me straight away? Of course, I'll help you look for him. Tell you what, you just come with me."

When I hesitated, she motioned me forward, saying "C'mon now. C'mon."

I shot one last look at the camper containing Pringle, then dawdled after her like a lost baby duckling.

"Now, normally I wouldn't offer up anything on my Chessy's behalf, but I like you and I have a feeling he will, too." She stopped outside her RV and waited for me to catch up. "Yes, that's right. C'mon inside."

Somewhat reluctantly, I followed Sharon into her camper, which stood parked somewhere between the camp manager's and the one that Charles and I had rented for the weekend.

And if Junetta's RV had been straight out of a 1980's fever dream, Sharon's was a futuristic space-scape. Everything inside was pristine and white and adorned with polished chrome accents. None of it had sharp edges. Instead, everything flowed seam-lessly from one piece into the next. On the sleek leather sofa sat an all-white cat with extra-long hair and stunning blue eyes.

Sharon waddled right over to him and tugged him into her arms. "Oh my sweet, sweet Chessy baby," she cooed.

"This place is amazing," I said on the wings of an exhale, still taking stock of the luxury camper and all its amenities. One of the walls sported an enormous TV, which was tuned in to the nature channel.

"Oh, this? It's Chester's world. I'm just lucky to live in it," Sharon prattled on.

I reached out to let the cat sniff my hand, and

he instantly began to purr. Wow, she even had the luxury cat model. Octo-Cat never treated me with such kindness, not even when he was at his happiest.

"I do mean that literally by the way," Sharon confided. When she shook her head, her pink cheeks jiggled. "Chester has all kinds of fe-fans on the social media. That's feline fans for the uninitiated. Now, when I started posting photos of our camping ad-ventures, one of those Hollywood types reached out to us via private message. One thing led to another, and now Chessy and I are going to be on reality TV. Filming starts this summer. They sent us this new house on wheels so we had time to get used to it before the show starts."

Wow, there was a lot to unpack there.

First off, why hadn't she led with this information? I'd have found her a lot more interesting if she had. After all, she was the first person I'd met— other than me—whose cat paid all the bills.

"Chester is such a talented kitty boy. Aren't you?" she continued to coo as she fawned over her feline life partner.

Pringle was going to die when he found out he'd been this close to a future reality TV star without ever actually meeting her. I couldn't wait to tell him.

"Angie?" Sharon stared at me with wide eyes and a concerned expression. I must have missed something.

"Have the police talked to you yet?" she said for what I guessed wasn't the first time.

"Yeah," I admitted, casting my eyes to the floor and discovering a luxe white marble with little glints of silver.

"Such a shame what happened to Junetta." She clucked her tongue and set the cat back on the sofa. "Why, she'd seemed entirely normal when I stopped off this morning to bring her my fresh-made and famous lingonberry pie."

My mind zoomed back to the scene I'd discovered earlier that afternoon. The pink-tinged vomit, the half-eaten pie. Mixed berry, I'd thought. But since I had no idea what a lingonberry was supposed to look like, that could very well have been what I'd seen.

Had Sharon just inadvertently confessed to the camp manager's murder? Yes, she liked to talk, but enough to accidentally slip up in such a major way?

I didn't know, and I was terrified of finding out.

Yes, suddenly I was very uncomfortable being alone with her in the RV...

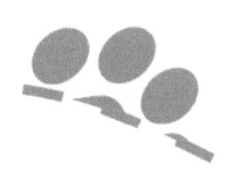

15

"have to go," I blurted out, but Sharon's wide body filled the passageway that led toward the door.

Her face turned down in a pout. "But you've only just gotten here."

"I have to find my cat. Remember?" I tried to push past her, but either she didn't get the hint or she didn't want to let me get away.

"Oh, look at me, so carried away with introductions that I plum forgot." She pressed her palm into her forehead and sighed. "Before you go, I have something for you."

The moment she turned to get whatever it was, I raced through the door and back out into the open where presumably no one would try to kill me while I was in plain sight of the others.

"I'm watching you!" the Airstream lady screamed from several lots away and shook her fist in the air.

I glanced at her briefly, then went running back toward Charles's and my camper.

At this point, I just wanted to go home and forget this whole day had ever happened, but I doubted the police would allow that while Charles and I were still under suspicion in an open investigation.

"There you are," Charles said from where he'd taken up in one of the chairs out-side our RV. "Angie, you're bright red. What's the matter?"

"Angie! Why'd you run off like that?" Sharon called, jogging to catch up.

A few other campers watched us and whispered to themselves.

A little girl with curly pigtails turned and hid her face against her father's leg. He stared daggers at me. This more than the interaction with the police made me feel very exposed and misunderstood.

Charles stood and wrapped an arm around me while Sharon finished her approach.

"Here," she said between gasps for air. It wasn't a long walk from her RV to ours, but I wasn't one to judge. Before Nan had forced me into morning runs with her and Cujo, I, too, would have been out of breath from the short jaunt.

When I tore my eyes away from Sharon, I looked down and saw a short, flat metal can resting on my palm.

"For your cat. I sure hope you find him." Sharon bent forward and took another deep breath, then left us to return to her own camper.

Charles took the can from me and read the label. "Albacore tuna. Huh."

"Tuna?" Pringle repeated from somewhere nearby.

"Pringle, where are you?" I whispered, scanning the area.

"Under here," the raccoon called quietly.

I got down on my hands and knees and peered into the darkness beneath the camper.

Two little hands reached out in supplication. "Tuna me, baby!"

"I'm going inside. If you want this, then maybe you should come inside, too." I huffed, then climbed back onto my feet and into the RV.

A moment later a thunk sounded from the bathroom.

"I'll get it," Charles announced as he paced across the living space.

As soon as the door clicked open, Pringle tore out of the bathroom in a manic fury. "Tuna, tuna, tuna," he chanted, jumping up beside me.

"You've been a very naughty raccoon."

He folded his hands in front of him and blinked up at me with large eyes. "What? Me?"

I scowled at him, ripping the can away when he tried to make a grab for it. "Yes, you. I told you to stay put."

"I did!" he squeaked. "See, I'm right here?"

"Then why did I spot you creeping into that other camper?"

Pringle took a step back. "Wh—?"

"Don't play stupid with me. I saw you."

"Okay, fine." When he sighed, his little shoulders rose and fell in defeat. "Okay, so maybe I was trying to solve the murder for you. Thing is, I want in on Pet Whisperer P.I., and I figured if I cracked this case single-handedly, you'd have no choice but to invite me to partner."

"Keep dreaming, ringworm," Octo-Cat snarled

before appearing as if out of no-where. He padded over to us, stretching each leg as he walked, making him look like some kind of bizarre circus act.

"And where were you?" I demanded, folding my arms over my chest, tuna still in hand.

A shudder wracked his striped body. "Hiding from that awful Sharon person."

"Ah, too bad you think she's so awful," I teased with a half-grin. "She brought a can of tuna for you, but seeing as you don't like her, I'm sure you don't want anything to do with—"

"Mine!" Octo-Cat cried, then batted the can from my hands and sent it crashing to the floor.

Both animals fell upon it at once, embroiled in a bitter fight for dominance.

"Do I even want to ask?" Charles pulled two bottles of soda from the mini fridge and handed one to me.

"Probably best that you didn't." I scooted over to make space for him on the sofa. "Did the police say anything more to you?"

"Not really. Although I was thinking you might want to change."

"Why?" I asked, a fresh wave of embarrassment washing over me as I remembered about my "juicy" booty.

He glanced down at my lap. "Well, the camp-ground manager was murdered with a poisonous pie, and you're covered in berry juice. Looks a little suspicious."

"Oh, I haven't told you yet. I know who made the pie." I loved sharing what I'd learned with him. Even though I'd been terrified at the time, now I was quite pleased with myself for gathering this little piece of intel.

He took a swig from his soda and then lowered the bottle. "Who?"

"Sharon," I revealed, pressing my lips in a tight line to keep from saying more.

He snorted and took another drink of soda. "But you don't think she's the one who did it, do you? I mean that's circumstantial evidence at best."

"Are you kidding? She totally did it," I said even though I still wasn't entirely convinced myself. I felt better having a primary suspect in mind rather than keeping the entire thing open-ended.

"I guess we'll see." Charles leaned forward and plucked the can of tuna away from the bickering animals, then went to stash it in the glove compart-ment where neither of them would be able to get it.

"No fair! No fair!" Pringle cried, jumping up and down in protest.

"Upchuck strikes again," Octo-Cat declared using his preferred nickname for whenever he was feeling irritated with my boyfriend.

"Where's that salmon?" I asked whoever was willing and able to answer.

"I left it outside, Charles replied, returning from the front and settling beside me on the sofa once again. "Couldn't very well bring it in here and stink up the rental."

"Look, how about this?" I attempted to reason with our furry stowaways. "If you two can be good for the rest of this weekend, I'll let you share that salmon."

"I don't want to share with him," they each cried in unison, sticking their tongue out at the other.

I shrugged as if none of it mattered to me. "That's my offer. Take it or go hungry. Frankly, I don't care what you do."

"Are you going to change?" Charles prompted, staring pointedly at my messy lap once more.

I sighed, knowing I didn't have any good options waiting for me in that suitcase. But he was right. Even if not for the incriminating berry stains, the outfit was decidedly filthy, thanks to our brief adventure in the woods.

Back in my room, I found a floor-length dress made of black crushed velvet. It had no back, which meant I couldn't wear a bra with it, but seeing as it was far less ostentatious than the other option—something that looked like a cast-off from the old film adaptation of Gone with the Wind—I pulled the garment over my head without giving it a second thought.

Of course, floor-length on Nan equated to mid-calf on me, but if anything, that just made it easier to move around in.

"You look amazing," Charles said, taking me in his arms when I exited the bed-room. He sang an old love song we both liked, and together we swayed between the kitchenette and the dining area.

"Ugh, get a room!" Octo-Cat cried when Charles bent down to kiss me.

"Get a life!" I shot back.

"I already have one. And she's currently right in my arms," Charles said, flashing me a debonair smile.

I giggled and rolled my eyes. But that was Charles for you. He made everything better, even an open murder investigation.

"Be right back," he said, letting go of me.

"Where are you going?" I pouted. I loved our impromptu dances and didn't want this one to end.

"If you're wearing this, then I've gotta change. I can't be camping while you're over here glamping it up," he said, then closed the door behind him.

16

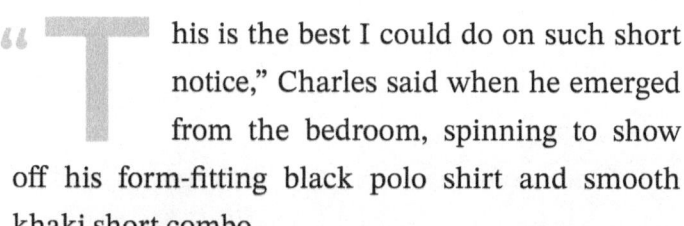

"This is the best I could do on such short notice," Charles said when he emerged from the bedroom, spinning to show off his form-fitting black polo shirt and smooth khaki short combo.

"Not exactly black tie, but I suppose black shirt will do." I giggled as he pulled me in for a hug. "Oh hey, I rummaged through our supplies a bit while you were changing and found a bottle of champagne. That gave me an idea."

Charles crossed to the mini fridge and grabbed the bottle by its neck, then reached into the cupboard and pulled out a box with two glass drinking flutes inside. "I was saving this for our last night out, but I guess we could have it now," he said with a shrug.

"No, don't open it yet!" I cried as he began to work at the foil top.

He paused, his shoulders tensing as he waited for me to reveal my big idea.

"We need to take it to Sharon's," I said.

Of course, he didn't get it. "What? Why?"

I put a hand on his waist and leaned in close. "As a means of entry. I'll apologize for being weird earlier, thank her for the tuna, and present the champagne."

He smiled now, coming around. "Yeah, and then what?"

"Well, we'll have Octo-Cat with us, too, and I'll ask her if her offer from earlier still stands. The one that involved coffee and gossip. She won't be able to resist. Once we're inside, you distract her while Octo-Cat and I talk to Chessy."

His brows pinched. "Chessy?"

"Her cat. If she really comes here as often as she says, then I bet Chessy has picked up on some gossip as well. He can also tell us if he noticed anything funny with Sharon earlier today."

"Like putting poison in a pie?" he suggested with a mischievous smile.

"Exactly." It might not be that easy, but given Sharon's penchant for gossip, it might not be that much harder, either.

"My girlfriend is so smart," Charles said, giving me a quick peck. "Do you think it matters that we only have two glasses?"

I pulled away from him. "I'll abstain. I need my wits about me anyway."

"There's one problem with your plan," Octo-Cat said from where he lay splayed across the sofa. "I'm not going."

I sat down beside him and attempted to stroke his fur, but he batted my hand away. "Please? You're kind of our ticket inside."

"I don't want to go, and you can't make me," he pouted, his expression sour.

But I knew how to get kitty to come out and play. "I still have that can of tuna, you know."

He turned his face away from me and mumbled, "If you're trying to bribe me, it won't work."

"Charles?" I said, holding my hand out.

Catching on immediately this time, he retrieve the can from the glove box and placed it on my hand, then went to the kitchenette and retrieved a crank-style can opener. He handed that to me, too.

As soon as the seal popped on the can, Octo-

Cat's tongue poked out of his mouth and his eyes grew wide. No cat could resist the sound—or the smell—of a freshly opened can, and that's exactly what I was counting on now.

"Just a small taste now, but you can go nuts once we're back," I said, waving the can around to entice him. "I promise we'll be as quick as possible."

"I'm not sharing with the raccoon," the tabby responded, unable to look away.

I glanced around the camper. Usually, the promise of food would send Pringle into a tailspin as well, but he was nowhere to be seen. Had probably snuck out to do some snooping again. The scamp.

"It's all yours, promise." I plucked the lid from the top of the can and grabbed a chunk of fish from inside. "In fact, here's your down payment."

Octo-Cat gobbled down the flaky morsel in a single breath. "Very well," he said after licking off his chops and tending to some light grooming ministrations.

"Can you put this somewhere Pringle can't get into it?" I asked Charles and went to wash my hands.

And then we were off.

Refusing to be carried in my arms, Octo-Cat trotted at my side.

Charles walked on my other side, hanging onto the wine and both glasses. I was also counting on the fact that Sharon wouldn't be able to resist him, given her flirtatious overtures earlier.

Sure enough, all the various pieces of my plan came together. It took almost no convincing at all for Sharon to welcome us into her home on wheels.

Inside, her best feline friend Chester lay curled up on the sofa, napping peacefully.

Octo-Cat took one look at him and turned his nose up. "Ugh, what a house pet."

Since we were in mixed company, I couldn't exactly point out that he was a house pet, too. Instead I kept quiet as Charles deftly maneuvered the conversation, seeking out a way to buy me some alone time with the cats.

After about five minutes of fawning over her luxury camper, Charles said, "I bet this baby has a massive cargo hold."

Sharon was quick to take the bait. "Oh, yes. It really does! C'mon. Let me show you."

My boyfriend turned to me with raised eyebrows.

I laughed and waved both him and Sharon off. "Go, go. You know that stuff isn't very interesting to me, anyway. Nope. Octo-Cat and I will just hang out in here and get to know Chester a bit better."

As soon as the door shut behind them, I nudged the white cat awake. "Chester, Chester. Sorry to bother you, but we need to talk."

His blue eyes blinked open slowly. "I must still be dreaming," he muttered to himself. "Otherwise I could have sworn there's a human here talking to me. Strange." He chuckled and then curled back up into a sleeping position.

"You better believe this is real and not a dream," Octo-Cat shouted, jumping up and getting right in the other cat's face. "This is my human, Angela, and she's special. She *can* talk to us."

Chester lifted his head slightly but appeared unimpressed.

Seeing as I didn't know how long Charles would be able to keep Sharon occupied outside, I cut right to the chase. "Chester, there's been a murder, and I was wondering if you know anything about it."

"No, I don't watch those channels," he said, craning his neck to look past me and stare at the TV on the far wall, which was still tuned in to the nature channel. "Sharon says they're a bad influence."

"She's not talking about TV. This is real life," Octo-Cat spat. Never mind that he also loved filling his days with TV and film. That is, when he wasn't napping, eating, or demanding ridiculous things of me.

"Who's been murdered, then? Not Sharon." Chester yawned and licked at his paw.

I sighed. "Sharon is fine. She was just here a second ago, remember? Anyway, the person who was murdered is named Junetta. She's the manager at this campground."

Chester watched a bird feed its young on the TV. "Which campground?" he asked absent-mindedly.

"This one," Octo-Cat hissed. "Yeesh, it's like you don't listen at all."

"I am listening," the white cat drawled. "But where are we? That's what I don't understand. Sharon and I travel back and forth so much, it's hard for me to keep track of where we are at any given time."

"Katahdin," I supplied.

"No, I don't know anyone by that name. I'm not allowed to leave the RV," Chester explained, although clearly misunderstanding. "So the only people I meet are the ones who come inside. Like you."

I decided to try a different tactic. "Sharon made a pie earlier today. Did you see her put anything into it?"

He shrugged. "The usual. Butter, eggs, flour, berries. Why are you so interested in the pie? It's not very good. Most humans don't even like it all that much."

"Did you—?" I began, but then the door swung open and Sharon's boisterous voice filled the space.

"If you decide to buy one of these beauties, give them my name. It just may get you a special deal."

"I'll do that," Charles promised, accepting a business card and gingerly placing it inside his wallet.

"Everything okay in here?" Charles asked when he spotted me on the couch with the two cats.

"Everything's just peachy keen," I said with a syrupy smile, even though it was the exact opposite of how I felt. We still didn't know whether Sharon was to blame, and even if I talked to Chester all night, I doubted I'd make any progress with him.

Well, Chester would be in for a rude awakening

once his reality show began filming. Something told me the producers wouldn't be content to film a lazy cat napping all day.

And here I'd always thought Octo-Cat was spoiled!

17

"Well, that got us exactly nowhere," I confided in Charles as we strolled back to our camper.

He grabbed my hand and pulled me into his side. "The police are here. Sooner or later, they'll figure this out. Why don't we just try to enjoy a relaxing night in?"

I chuffed at this notion. "Relaxing went out the window several hours ago. Besides, if the police are still here, then they may come back to ask us more questions."

"Let's try not to worry about that until it happens," Charles said softly. "Hey, we're all dressed up with only one place to go. Let's have some dinner and just enjoy each other's company. We can still enjoy what's left of this vacation. It's not too late."

I blinked up at the darkening sky. It had already been such a long and exhausting day. "Can we finish watching the movie from last night?" I asked, thinking back to the happy little cartoon characters.

Charles sucked air in through his teeth. "Oooh. Again? We already finished that."

I jabbed a finger at this chest. "You finished it. I fell asleep."

He laughed at my bluster. "And what makes you think you won't fall asleep again?" he asked, but as soon as we returned to the trailer, he started up the show for me.

And, yes, Charles was correct.

I fell asleep fairly early in.

He woke me up to eat a dinner that he'd prepared while I dozed. We watched some more.

And then I fell asleep again.

Charles must have carried me to bed, because that's where I was when I woke up with a chittering raccoon on my chest.

"Pringle," I whispered in irritation. "Go away!"

"Hey, lady. I solved the murder," he ground out,

wiggling his fingers in a silly jazz hands maneuver. "Come with me. I'll tell you everything, then you can go back to sleep. Cross my heart."

I glanced over to Charles who was still sleeping peacefully tucked in tight beneath the comforter. Gosh, I loved him so much. He didn't deserve the level of crazy I regularly brought to our lives. Yet what would I do without him? He was my rock in a world of sand.

"Make it quick," I grumbled, grabbing my robe and tying it tight around me, then shoving my bare feet into sneakers before following the raccoon out of the camper.

Other than a few scattered interior lights and the stars above, the campground lay obscured in complete darkness. Luckily, I always had my phone on me—a force of habit—so I clicked into the flashlight app and used it to illuminate my steps.

"Where are you taking me?" I called after Pringle as he scampered ahead.

"Almost there," he called back, moving faster and faster. We walked for a long time.

But despite my questions, Pringle didn't explain, and he didn't stop. Not until we reached a large clearing in the woods where half a dozen wooden tables had been set out for picnickers.

"It's okay. You can come out now!" Pringle called into the night.

I shone my light toward the tree line just in time to see the massive grizzly crawl out to join us in the clearing.

Oh my!

I'd been so caught up in Junetta's murder that I'd completely forgotten about poor Gloria and her plea for help. I was just about to tell her that—and to apologize for not being able to help—when a bullet whizzed past me and lodged itself in a thick tree trunk a few feet behind and to the side of Gloria.

I spun and saw a man, probably about sixty years of age, holding a smoking hunting rifle. "Get back!" he cried. "There's a wild grizzly on the loose!"

"It's okay. I'm okay!" I said, raising my arms to show him I meant no harm. "And she's not on the loose. This is her home."

Oh, how I prayed that both Gloria and Pringle had the good sense to remain hidden while I dealt with this gun-toting lunatic.

"Why do you have a gun? This is a protected nature park," I reminded him rather pedantically.

"For safety and maybe for revenge," he growled back. "Who are you?"

Uh-oh. I did not like the sound of this one bit.

Still, I tried my best to keep my voice calm. "I'm Angie. My boyfriend and I are staying at the campground. We only just got here today. Who are you?"

"Carl. I came as soon as I heard about Junetta's passing. I loved her, you know? And whoever killed her is going to pay big time."

Carl must be the ex-husband Sharon had mentioned, the crazy one who still came around from time to time to try to win her back.

"Well, Carl." I paused and licked my lips. Suddenly they felt so very dry. "I want justice for Junetta, too," I continued. "I'm the one who discovered her body."

I expected him to yell and snarl at me, to demand answers I didn't have to give, but instead the old man let out a strangled cry and sank to the ground.

The gun clattered at his feet but didn't go off.

I swooped in and grabbed it, then stood by idly as Carl cried his heart out. I had a million and one questions in that moment. Like why Pringle had brought me here and what Gloria had to do with it. But I had no doubts as to whether the weeping man in front of me was innocent. The man was simply too torn up about his ex's passing to be the culprit.

As Carl's sobs grew more and more muted, I heard Pringle and Gloria's voices rise into the night.

"He brought the exploding lightning," Gloria whispered in anguish. "He tried to aim it at me. If I die, my cubs won't make it on their own. Please, Pringle, you have to help us. It's getting so dangerous here, but where else can we go?"

"Relax, lady," the raccoon said with his signature lack of empathy. "My human sidekick and I nearly have this figured out. You and the tikes will be fine. Raccoon's honor."

I glanced over to Carl, trying to determine if he'd heard the animals calling out. But he was so lost in his own sorrow that he didn't even notice me look his way.

And so I took a chance, keeping the rifle gripped tightly in my hands, and crept deeper into the woods. I'd switched off my phone's light, which meant I had to rely on my other senses to guide me.

"Pringle? Gloria?" I whispered as I treaded over dry leaves and loose twigs.

"Over here," the raccoon called from somewhere nearby.

"I can't see anything," I whispered back. "Can you come to me?"

"I'm here," Pringle said from much closer now. "But the bear went back to be with her babies."

"What's going on? You said you figured out the murder?"

He let out a huff. "Well, I thought I had, but something tells me I got it all wrong."

"What was your theory?" I begged.

"So when we first met Gloria, she mentioned how her mate had tried to kill their cubs and that she was on the lam. Then I figured any guy who would kill his own kids could easily off a human," he said. I couldn't see him, but I imagined him making big sweeping gestures to emphasize his assumed brilliance.

Unfortunately, I had to burst his bubble. "But that makes no sense," I said in exasperation.

"Of course it makes sense." Hurt echoed in his voice. I loved that he was trying to help, but one of us could have been shot back there. This was serious business, and I needed him to take it as such.

"The murder weapon was a poison pie," I reminded him with a sigh. "Do you know any bears who can bake?"

"Hey, I could bake if I wanted to."

"Well, you never have, and also you're not a bear. Is that why you brought me out here?"

"I wanted to tell you and Gloria at the same time. That way I could get my second salmon and make partner in the P.I. firm in one nice combo move." He sounded completely chastised now, which meant it would be the wrong time to point out that he wouldn't be joining Octo-Cat's and my business any time in the near future.

"So you told Gloria to meet us here?" I prompted.

"Yeah. Yeah, I did. I just had to go and get you first."

Now that the shock of meeting Carl had worn off, something important clicked together in my mind. "I overheard the two of you talking about exploding lightning. Gloria wasn't talking about fireworks like I thought before. She was talking about guns. There are illegal hunters in the area. If Junetta figured that out, she could have put a stop to it. Someone didn't want that to happen, though."

"Yeah, I guess that makes sense," Pringle agreed.

Yes, yes, we were on to something here. We could still solve this thing.

"Pringle, I need your expert snooping skills," I said, hoping I wouldn't later come to regret it. "Do you think you can help me close this case?"

He pumped his arm and made a terrible honking noise, then shouted, "Okay! Let's hit the road, sweetheart!"

Of course, he happily agreed.

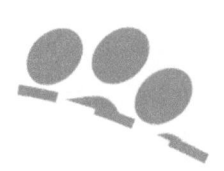

18

By the time I got back to the picnic area, Carl had already gotten up and left.

Shoot. I still had some questions I wanted to ask him, but I'd have to worry about that later.

Pringle went to find Gloria so that he could explain our plan and to promise we'd do something about the illegal hunting as soon as we found some answers. Much to his chagrin, I also made him tell the grizzly that a second payment would not be needed, that we were happy to help simply out of the kindness of our hearts.

While he took care of that, I sat at one of the picnic tables with the rifle laid out on its surface and called Charles to tell him what had happened and what Pringle and I were planning next.

Luckily, Pringle liked guns—although his primary experience was in handling the Nerf variety. Still, he was excited to implement the plan exactly as I'd laid it out. And if there was one thing I'd learned about working with animals in all my time as a pet whisperer, it was that the best results came when you got them to act on their natural behavior. Pringle loved collecting secrets via his snooping endeavors, and I'd already caught him slipping into RVs undetected earlier that day. In fact, that's how this whole adventure started in the first place.

So now when I asked him to keep doing it, he readily agreed. The plan involved him sneaking into the campers parked at the grounds and searching for rifles or any other hunting paraphernalia. Once we found out who all might be engaged in illegal hunting, we could narrow down our suspect list.

First, though, I needed him to pay a quick visit to Junetta's camper and find the logbook Charles had mentioned to the police. She'd recorded our arrival, which meant she had likely recorded everyone else's, too.

Pringle made quick work of this first task and

delivered the logbook to me and Charles, even taking care to set it down nicely and turn to the page we needed so that neither of us would get our fingerprints on it.

"Charles," I said after studying the logbook for a few minutes. "Do you remember the name of the woman who accused me of killing Junetta?"

He thought for a moment. "We never got her first name, but the police officers referred to her as Ms. Stevens."

I nodded. That's what I had thought, too. "She's not in here," I said, chewing on my lip.

Charles read through each line, then swore under his breath. "You're right. What do you think it means?"

"Octo-Cat," I called. "Come here. We need your help for a second."

He groaned but got up and hopped onto the table. "What do you need, your majesty?"

"Can you turn the page for us?" I asked, letting his insult slide. "Go back to the older entries."

"Smart," Charles said bumping his shoulder into mine. "No prints."

Octo-Cat struggled with the task but eventually got the page turned.

I read through that page but still found no mention of Ms. Stevens's check-in.

"Again, please," I asked my cat.

It took three more turns of the page before we finally found an entry for a Miss Sara Stevens. The entry was made so long ago that it was in a different handwriting. She'd been here even longer than Junetta had. *Hmmm.*

Charles pulled out his phone and opened the Notes app. "I'm making a list," he said as he typed furiously on the tiny keyboard. "Every lot number and the date of the most recent check-in."

While he did that, I jotted down any names that occurred multiple times—identifying the grounds' frequent visitors, people like Sharon.

Octo-Cat helped us turn the pages as needed, but not without the promise of many, many lobster rolls, shrimp kebabs, and cans of tuna in his future.

When Pringle returned, he looked absolutely exhausted. I poured him a dish of water and waited for him to catch his breath before asking for a recap.

"Well?" I prompted when he still hadn't shared his findings with the group.

"Twenty-two RVs," he said, sucking in a deep, dramatic breath, even though he'd had more than enough time to recover. "I was able to break into seventeen of them. Of those, four had rifles and two had handguns."

"Do you remember which ones?" I prompted, after relaying this info to Charles.

"Do I remember?" he spat. "Of course, I remember."

"Then show me."

Pringle scampered around telling me what he'd found in each RV as well as identifying which ones he couldn't open. I jotted it all down in a series of text messages to Charles so he could check the occupancy periods for each of our gun owners on the premises.

As Pringle approached the end of the line, I pointed to Sara Stevens's aqua-accented Airstream. "What about this one? Did it have a gun?"

"No gun, but lots and lots of ammo. I found trail maps, too, with paths marked in red," he said, unwittingly revealing our smoking gun.

Just then the door to the Airstream flew open, and Sara Stevens stepped out in a robe not entirely dissimilar to my own. "What are you doing out here?" she shouted, then pointed at Pringle. "And what is that thing?"

Another camper door opened and a man and

woman wearing matching flannel pajama bottoms exited from it.

"Go get Charles," I muttered to Pringle from the side of my mouth.

He saluted, then scampered off.

"Not going to answer me?" Her face was red, her eyes wild. "Then I'm calling the cops. I'm sure they'll just love coming back out after spending half the day with us."

She grabbed her phone and punched in the number.

"That's enough, Sara," a man said. "This is a public campground, not your private property."

Sara stood on tiptoe trying to see past me in search of the voice. Even with that added bit of height, she wasn't tall enough, though.

"Is that you, Carl?" she called out. "Don't be fooled by her pretty face. This woman murdered Junetta today, murdered her in cold blood!"

Aww, she thought I was pretty. Not that that made me despise her any less.

Sara lifted up her phone and shouted, "Do you hear that? I have a murderer sneaking around outside my camper. Come and get her, boys."

"Funny, from what I understand Angie only just arrived here today," Carl pointed out.

Sara ended the call with humph and thrust her phone back into her robe pocket. "Yes, and an hour later Junetta was dead. Coincidence? I think not."

"I didn't kill her," I insisted for what felt like the hundredth time. This time my confession of innocence was more for the benefit of the other campers who had come out to gawk at our confrontation. "Someone poisoned her with a pie, and I don't know the first thing about baking."

A gasp sounded across the way. "With my pie?" Sharon cried, waddling over in a hurry. "The secret ingredient is love, not poison. Never poison."

Behind Sharon, I spotted Charles striding over. This gave me all the courage I needed to trot my theory out for all to hear.

"The pie wasn't poisoned when you gave it to her," I called to Sharon, then fixed my gaze directly on Sara Stevens. "Someone added it in after the fact. Someone who's been around for a bit and knows all about Junetta's open door policy."

I paused to gauge everyone's reaction, but no one said a thing. Charles was at my side now, standing in a silent show of support.

And so I continued. "And Junetta wasn't murdered in cold blood. Her death was planned. Somebody was very unhappy with her. From what I can gather, she might not have been the best campground manager, but she was learning on the job. And recently she'd learned all about an illegal hunting ring operating right here under her nose. She planned to put an end to it, to make sure the guilty parties were held accountable. But they silenced her before she could say a thing."

"She knew." Carl's voice cracked and he hung his head. "This whole time, she knew. Oh! This is all my fault!"

"So you confess!" Sara shouted and pointed. "Filthy scum, no wonder Junetta left you."

"No, no, it wasn't me. I would have never…" His words fell away as he stumbled backward.

Catching him in a weak moment, Sara pounced. "You killed her. It makes perfect sense. You couldn't have her, so you decided no one could."

"When Junetta found out I'd been coming out here to hunt illegally, she was so upset. That was the beginning of the end for us."

"You came here?" I prompted, even though I was already pretty sure I knew what he would say next.

Carl pumped his head. "Yes, I came here many times over the past couple years. The animals aren't expecting it, so they're easy shots. I'd bring Junetta with me on my trips sometimes, but never tell her where I was going after dark. I guess that's why she came after the divorce, why she decided to take a job here. She thought it was just me hunting out here. She didn't know there were more of us. Didn't know who made it so that local law enforcement didn't catch on."

"Who was in charge, Carl?" I asked. "Who made it all possible?"

"She was your friend!" he shouted at Sara. "Why would you do this?"

The accused took a giant step back and pressed herself against her Airstream. "I... I don't know what you're talking about."

"It's easy to blame others when you're trying to cover your own back," I said, taking a step toward the cornered killer.

"You! You can't prove anything," she spat at me.

"Oh, but I can," Carl said, taking out his phone and jiggling it at her. "I kept a record of every hunt, names and all. You're in it everywhere. Won't be difficult to match you up to the timeline, especially since I saw you at the center when I last went to buy ammunition. When I heard that Junetta was poisoned, I called my friend who works there, and they confirmed you bought a weed killer that day - one that is highly toxic to humans."

"Go away! This is my home, and you're not welcome here!" Sara shouted, completely losing it now.

"You're going to jail. For Junetta's sake, I hope you rot in there," Carl hissed.

More and more campers overheard the yelling and came outside to investigate. The police arrived a short while later to take things over. And the hysterical killer was the one who had called them herself.

ith Junetta's killer behind bars, Charles and I headed back to our little home on wheels for the weekend. Pringle and Octo-Cat had made themselves scarce, allowing us to cash in on some much-needed relaxation.

We slept in late the next morning, then ate our way through a massive stack of messy, syrupy pancakes in bed. It was bliss.

"If we don't go anywhere, we can't be forced out of relaxation mode," I reasoned, and Charles agreed enthusiastically.

"I still feel bad about dragging you all the way out here only to have the worst weekend ever," he said with a slight frown pulling down the corner of his mouth.

I pushed my last bite of pancakes around the edges of my plate to collect the remaining drips of syrup, then shoved the whole thing in my mouth and sighed with delight. "Well, it was a pretty bad Friday," I said once I'd managed to swallow down that heavenly bite. "But the weekend as a whole has yet to be determined."

Octo-Cat, who lay cuddled at our feet, popped his head up and said, "Life with Angela is often irritating, but it's never boring."

I decided not to translate that for Charles.

"Hey, should we grill up that salmon for lunch?" he asked with a laugh.

"Are you kidding me? It's been sitting out since yesterday. The thing is probably covered in flies by now."

"Actually, I already took care of that," Pringle announced, standing in the doorway with one paw to the wall. "Sorry. I know I was supposed to let you have it as a way of saying sorry for ruining your picnic, but I was just so hungry after all that sneaking around I did on your behalf. You know how it goes."

I nodded and set my polished-off plate at the

end of the bed. "I do, and it's okay. We weren't going to eat it, anyway."

Pringle cast his eyes toward the floor, then grabbed the tip of his tail and began grooming it nervously with his fingers. "Sure, but I still feel really... I don't know... sick to my stomach. It's weird."

"That feeling is guilt," I supplied with a lazy grin. "You feel bad about ruining our picnic, but really, it's okay. I'm not mad."

"If you're not mad, then why do I still feel this way? How can I make it stop?" He pouted and began to twist his tail in his hands.

"Really, it's—"

"Oh, I've got it!" Pringle shouted, then turned and ran off. When he returned, he jumped up onto the bed and climbed onto my lap. His little black fist was closed tight around something, but I couldn't see what.

"I've been feeling sick like this for a while now, and I think it all started after Chucky and I helped those seagulls," he said, pointing toward Charles with his free hand. I was definitely not okay with him nicknaming my boyfriend after a demonic horror doll, but seeing as Pringle was attempting a genuine, heartfelt moment here, I let it slide.

Instead I asked, "What's wrong with the seagulls?"

"Nothing's wrong exactly. But Charles helped with that case, and I didn't share the payment. I thought it's what I wanted, but I hate feeling this way. So..." He opened his palm to reveal a sparkling diamond solitaire.

I gasped, completely taken by surprise. "What? Where did you get that?"

"The seagulls gave it to us, remember? I always keep it nearby, since it's one of my greatest treasures."

"It's been here all weekend? Where?" I glanced around the room. This RV was packed so tight I had no idea where Pringle may have made his secret stash.

"Don't worry about that. If I give up all my good hiding spots, I'll feel sick for a different reason." He attempted a smile, but it looked wrong, thanks to all those sharp little teeth. "So do you forgive me?"

"Of course, I forgive you, Pringle." I reached out and patted his head. Pringle wasn't a domesticated animal and didn't like it when I touched him, but I felt like I had to do something to connect with him in that moment.

He winced at my touch, then straightened his

posture and pressed the ring into my hand. "Then here. Do with it what you will."

"I have a feeling this is going to get real gross, real fast," Octo-Cat droned as he jumped off the bed. "Come find me when you want to feed me."

Pringle disappeared after him, leaving my boyfriend and I on our own. We both stared at the ring, neither saying anything. Talk about opening a giant can of worms.

When at last I couldn't take the awkward silence any longer, I giggled and joked, "So you wanna get married or something?"

But Charles didn't laugh. Not even a little. Instead he cleared his throat and got out of bed.

"No, no, come back. I'm sorry!" I called after him. Me and my big mouth. *Stupid, stupid, stupid.*

He rooted around in his luggage, then climbed into bed beside me, holding out both hands in fists. "Pick one," he said.

I tapped on his right fist, and he opened it up to reveal a little satin box.

My breathing hitched as I looked from the ring in my hand to the box in his. "Charles, I..."

"Open it," he said with a soft smile, watching me so closely I doubt he blinked at all.

Delicately, I lifted the lid to reveal a princess-cut

diamond surrounded by a tight outcropping of amethysts.

"I planned to ask you this weekend. On our picnic actually, but then..." He sighed and watched me with wide eyes. "Well... you know the rest."

"Are you really asking me—?"

"To marry me? Yes." He sat up higher in bed and grabbed both of my hands in his. "This isn't how I'd planned it, but I love you, Angie Russo. For better or worse. No matter what. Do you love me like that, too?"

"Yes, I do," I said as he took the ring out of the box and slipped it onto my finger. "And yes, I will marry you."

I wiggled my fingers, delighting in the heft of my new prized accessory, at the way it sparkled in the light. Then I reached for Charles's hand and slipped the seagull's ring onto his pinky finger.

"A perfect fit," I said. "Just like us."

"Just like us," he agreed.

We shared our first kiss as a betrothed couple, and then I pulled away and asked, "What would you have done if I picked the other hand?"

My fiancé's eyes flashed with mischief. "Hmm, I guess we'll never know," he teased, and then kissed me again.

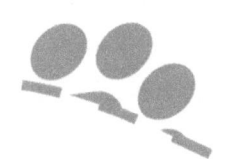

20

W hen we returned home Sunday evening, my entire family stood waiting on the porch.

"Congratulations, Mr. and Mrs. Charles Longfellow the Third!" Nan cried, setting off a party popper.

"I have a new daddy!" her Chihuahua Paisley barked happily.

My mother and father rushed down the steps to greet us, exchanging hugs and congratulations.

Octo-Cat hopped out of the camper and groaned. "Remind me again why you thought it would be a good idea to bring a cat on a camping trip?"

"It wasn't our idea," I muttered and rolled my

eyes. Knowing my luck, the tabby would punish me for this sleight for many months to come—and it hadn't even been my fault.

"I missed you, Octavius!" Paisley squeaked, then slathered him in kisses.

"Get off me, you demented creature," he growled.

Paisley pinned him down and took great care cleaning out each of his ears.

"Okay, okay. I've missed you too, you little scalawag," Octo-Cat acquiesced. He even stopped struggling as Paisley continued to pepper him with sloppy puppy kisses.

While everyone's attention was on the cat and dog, the raccoon exited the RV the same way he'd initially entered, through the bathroom vent up top. "If anyone needs me, I'll be in my tree house, starting my third watch-through of the cult reality classic *Survivor*."

I turned away from my parents and called out to him. "Pringle, wait. Come inside and join us for dinner. I'm sure Nan has something wonderful prepared."

Nan's face lit up. "I sure do. We're having blackened salmon and risotto."

My stomach turned at the mention of salmon, but I worked hard to keep my face light and happy.

"Sounds delicious." Charles threaded his fingers through mine and then raised our joined hands and pressed a kiss to them.

"Everything's ready. Just step inside." Nan guided us back into the house. "I even brought out the good china. Why, it's not every day my favorite granddaughter gets engaged."

"And it's not today, either," I pointed out with a chuckle. "We got engaged yesterday."

"Oh, hush, you." But Nan laughed, too.

Pringle scampered in after us and climbed up onto the table.

"Manners," Nan said, fixing him with a stern look.

He hesitated before climbing down onto one of the chairs. His face barely cleared the surface of the table, the cutie.

"I'll go get you a booster," I said, heading toward the entry closet where Nan kept all kinds of strange knickknacks. I wouldn't be surprised if I found a booster chair there, too.

A light tapping at the door drew my attention away.

I opened it up and found Bravo and Abigull

standing on the porch together. "Hi, guys. What's up?"

"Angie, Angie," the young bird cawed. "We found her!"

I was almost afraid to ask. Mostly because I already knew the answer. "Found who?"

"Your long-lost grandmother," Bravo confirmed. "She hasn't left the state. Just moved. We found her somewhere in the middle."

"Near Mount Katahdin?" I ventured.

"Affirmative," Bravo squawked.

"How did you know?" Abigull asked, tilting her head to the side.

I let out a tired sigh. "Because with the way my life has gone lately, it just makes sense."

"We can take you to her. Are you ready?" the elder seagull asked.

"I'd like that very much, but first I have a dinner engagement. Can you come back tomorrow?"

When both birds agreed, I said goodbye and rejoined my family in the dining room. There would be time to tell them all about the seagulls' discovery later.

Tonight, we would celebrate.

Tomorrow, we could chase after our next big mystery.

Are you ready to go back on the road with Angie, Octo-Cat, and crew?

Get your copy of *Persian Penalty* so that you can keep reading this series today!

* * *

Pssst... If you absolutely loved this book and want even more, make sure you **sign up for Molly's newsletter**. When you do, you'll receive an exclusive digital prize pack, including a free book!

WHAT'S NEXT?

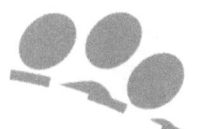

We've finally found my long-lost grandmother, and I refuse to wait another day to meet her in person. Unfortunately, she's proving rather difficult to pin down.

So Charles and I decide to finish our search on the ground and book a quirky lakeside B&B to serve as our HQ while we're in the area.

But because nothing is ever easy, we stumble across mystery after mystery while simply trying to get a good night's sleep. Precious items from our luggage keep going missing, the door to our room won't close properly, and bad reviews online hint at even worse things to come. Of course, the ill-tempered proprietress and her even crazier Persian cat refuse to help—or even to apologize.

All of which makes me wonder, will I finally get to meet my missing grandma face-to-face, or could the trouble at the inn have us packing our bags long before then?

PERSIAN PENALTY is now available.

Get your copy so that you can keep reading this series today!

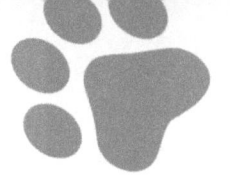

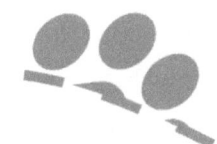

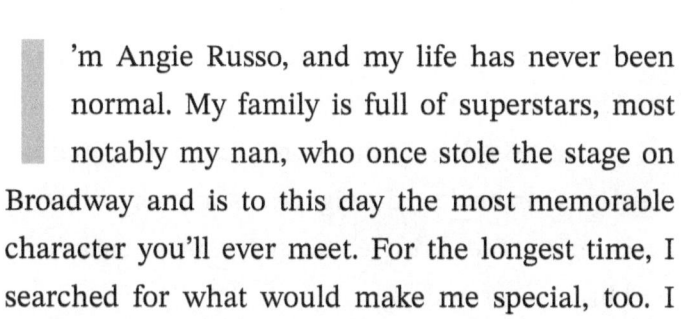

'm Angie Russo, and my life has never been normal. My family is full of superstars, most notably my nan, who once stole the stage on Broadway and is to this day the most memorable character you'll ever meet. For the longest time, I searched for what would make me special, too. I guess that's why I racked up seven associate degrees before finally settling into a career.

My calling was actually a cat call—no, not the sleazy, random-guy-on-the-street kind. An actual *meow*. A meow that I heard loud and clear, and in English of all things.

Yes, I can talk to animals. Just call me Miss Dolittle.

I was working as a paralegal when a will

meeting went awry. One thing led to another, and I got zapped by a faulty coffee maker, lost consciousness, and then eventually woke up with a talking cat on my chest.

And, boy, did he have a lot of demands!

Fast-forward a couple years, and now he's my partner in the P.I. business. Thanks in large part to his former owner, his name is Octavius Maxwell Ricardo Edmund Frederick Fulton Russo, Esq, P.I. Since that's way longer than any honest name should be, I've taken to calling him Octo-Cat.

Together, we live in a beautiful manor home not too far from Blueberry Bay in Maine. Nan lives with us, too, as does her syrupy sweet rescue Chihuahua, Paisley. Our backyard neighbor is a sticky-fingered raccoon named Pringle; he helps us occasionally and bribes us regularly.

Never a dull moment with this colorful cast of sidekicks.

Of course, I'd be remiss if I failed to mention Charles Longfellow, III. He's the senior partner at a local law firm, the same one I used to work at back in the day. He's my boyfri—I mean, *fiancé!*

He's my fiancé!

Wow, I still haven't gotten used to saying that.

He proposed to me on a surprise weekend

getaway that came with a rented RV and a crazy murder mystery. It was supposed to help me relax, but I'm honestly more wound up than ever.

Not just because of the proposal, but also because of what happened after we returned home.

A few months ago I made a deal to help some seagulls with an inter-flock dispute. In exchange, they promised to find my long-lost grandmother, whom I only knew about thanks to a hidden letter Pringle filched from the attic.

Nan—my best friend and the woman who raised me while my parents were busy focusing on their careers and each other—well, it turns out she's not actually blood related.

I'm still getting over the shock from that partic-ular revelation!

Needless to say, Nan has had a rough time accepting that I want to connect to the grand-mother I never knew. I've taken every opportunity I can to reassure her, but it's still hard. She didn't choose for her best friend—my blood grandfather—to hand her his baby and ask her to run. Nan never asked why, and he died before I could suss out any answers. That leaves my long-lost grandmother as the only one who can explain why things happened the way they did.

I've got to find her and learn more about my family's secret past. Yes, I've considered that she might be dangerous, especially considering the great lengths old grandpa went to get my mother away from her.

But I'm pretty sure I can handle a confrontation with an octogenarian, no matter how intimidating she may be.

Anyway, I tell you all this now because the seagulls have finally located my secret grandmother just outside of Katahdin.

And I'm preparing to go meet her for the first time ever. I'm so excited, I can hardly—

Deep breaths.

Okay, I'm scared out of my mind, but that doesn't mean I'm going to pass up this opportunity. I mean, it's like pulling off a bandage, right? I just have to do it if I ever expect the wound beneath to heal.

I stumbled into the kitchen, practically tripping over my oversized slippers as I moved from the hardwood of the dining room to the tile in the kitchen.

"Good morning," Nan sang, floating over and

pushing a banana-nut muffin into my hand. "I'll put the coffee on now."

"Thanks," I murmured, shoving the muffin in the general direction of my mouth, and hoping it would end up in the right place. I'd never been a morning person. Even less so since developing my fear of electric coffee makers.

Don't judge. I'm sure if you ever got electrocuted, you'd fear the appliance that attacked you, too.

I'd tried a million different caffeine solutions from canned coffee to instant powder, and most recently a French press. Nothing beat the freshly brewed stuff, though. It was the whole experience, really. The smell, the sound, all of it.

Thankfully, Nan was only too happy to aid in my addiction.

And so I munched on my baked good while she tidied up the kitchen and the coffee brewed. When it finished, Nan poured me a cup and mixed a bit of pumpkin spice flavored creamer in. It was one of her greatest joys to discover PSL off season, which meant it was always in season for me.

She allowed me to take a few life-giving sips before attempting a conversation. Smart woman.

"What have you got planned for today, dear?"

she asked, pouring a cup for herself, and then drifting toward the living room.

I dutifully followed, shuffling my feet so that the little kitty heads on my slippers shook with each motion. Nan had purchased them for me as a Valentine's gift, remarking how much the plush felines looked like Octo-Cat. I now wore them most days, partially because it made Nan happy and partially because it bugged my cat to no end.

"I should get slippers with little human heads attached. See how you like it," the tabby muttered from atop the sofa, his tail flicking in tell-tale irritation.

I took a seat in my favorite armchair while Nan settled herself on the couch. Paisley hopped up beside her and shoved her wet little puppy nose into Octo-Cat's rear end.

"Ick!" he shouted as the hair on his back went up. "Why must you always sniff me there? Surely, the scent hasn't changed from yesterday!"

"Good morning, big brother!" the little dog squealed. She wagged her tail so hard, her whole body shook from the effort.

Octo-Cat growled and ran away to hide.

And so went our morning routine.

"Dear?" Nan prompted, casting a quizzical glance my way. "Your plans for today?"

Oh! Oh, right.

"Sorry. The pets were distracting me," I mumbled to buy myself some time. Now that I had enough caffeine in my system to form a few coherent thoughts, I realized what I needed to do, and it was the very thing I'd been dreading all night. No wonder I was so tired this morning.

"Nan?" I asked, fixing my eyes on the mug in my hands as I continued. "Bravo visited last night. He's found my bio grandmother."

"Oh," she said simply.

When I glanced up again, she had her gaze fixed on an indeterminable point in the distance and sat stroking Paisley without really seeing her—or me.

"Nan?" I prompted again. I hated that she felt this way, but I also couldn't live with myself if I didn't at least try to meet the woman who had birthed my mother. Whether she'd been part of our lives or not, she was still an important part of who my mother and I had become.

Nan sighed gently. "I suppose you'll want to go meet her, then."

"Yes," I answered firmly. That was not up for

debate, no matter how much Nan disliked the idea. But I had a plan to soften the blow...

I waited for her eyes to meet mine, and then I flashed her a reassuring smile. "I want you to come with me."

PERSIAN PENALTY is now available.

Get your copy so that you can keep reading this series today!

ABOUT MOLLY FITZ

While *USA Today bestselling* author Molly Fitz can't technically talk to animals, she and her three feline writing assistants have deep and very animated conversations as they navigate their days.

She lives with her child and their own private zoo somewhere in the wilds of Alaska. Molly will occasionally venture out for good food, great coffee, or to meet new animal friends.

Learn more about Molly and her books, and be sure to sign up for her newsletter at **www.Molly Mysteries.com**.

ALSO BY MOLLY FITZ

Learn more about Molly's collected works, so that you can decide which book you'd like to read next...

PET WHISPERER P.I.

Angie Russo just partnered up with Blueberry Bay's first ever talking cat detective. Along with his ragtag gang of human and animal helpers, Octo-Cat is determined to save the day... so long as it doesn't interfere with his schedule.

Start with book 1, ***Kitty Confidential***.

MERLIN'S MAGICAL MYSTERIES

Gracie Springs is not a witch... but her cat is. Now she must help to keep his secret or risk spending the rest of her life in some magical prison. Too bad trouble seems to find them at every turn!

Start with book 1, ***Merlin Takes a Familiar***.

PARANORMAL TEMP AGENCY

Tawny Bigford's simple life takes a turn for the magical when she stumbles upon her landlady's murder and is recruited by a talking black cat named Fluffikins to take over the deceased's role as the official Town Witch for Beech Grove, Georgia.

Start with book 1, ***Witch for Hire***.

THE MYSTERIES OF MOONLIGHT MANOR (WITH TRIXIE SILVERTALE)

Sydney Coleman has it all—until she doesn't. No sooner does she launch her bed and breakfast, than a trio of ghosts turn up oppose her at every turn. They insist she solve the murder of their mistress, but Sydney is desperate for cash. If she can't book some guests fast, her haunted mansion is utterly doomed.

Start with book 1, ***Moonlight & Mischief***.

CONNECT WITH MOLLY

Sign up for my newsletter and get a special digital prize pack for joining, including an exclusive story, *Meowy Christmas Mayhem*, fun quiz, and lots of cat pictures!

Sign up: **MollyMysteries.com/subscribe**

Now, if you ever wished you could converse with cats, here's your opportunity! This is me officially inviting you into my whacky inner world as part of my Cozy Kitty Book Club.

For those who just can't get enough of my zany cat characters and their hapless humans, this book club will provide new content to devour and the chance to get to know my best author friends.

From exclusive stories, behind-the-scenes trivia to never-before-released bonus content, and monthly giveaways, there's a lot to love about the Cozy Kitty Book Club. Join today to find out what we're reading next!

Join: **MollyMysteries.com/club**